TINY HOUSE, BIG LOVE

OLIVIA DADE

Copyright © 2019 by Olivia Dade

All rights reserved.

No part of this book may be reproduced in any form or by any electronic or mechanical means, including information storage and retrieval systems, without written permission from the author, except for the use of brief quotations in a book review.

ISBN: 978-1-945836-07-7

❦ Created with Vellum

ABOUT TINY HOUSE, BIG LOVE

On camera. Up close. In denial—but not for much longer…

After a relationship gone bad, Lucy Finch is leaving everything behind. Her old home, her old job, her old insecurities. Even Sebastián Castillo, her protective but intensely private friend of almost twenty years. Before she moves halfway across the country, though, she has one last request for Seb: She wants him to help her choose a tiny house on cable television. And maybe during the filming process, she can discover once and for all whether his feelings for her are more than platonic…

Sebastián would rather do anything than appear on HATV. But Lucy needs him, and he can't say no. Not when she's about to leave, taking his heart with her. Hiding how he feels with a television crew watching their every move will prove difficult, though—especially when that crew is doing their sneaky best to transform two longtime friends into a couple.

Tiny spaces. Hidden emotions. The heat generated by decades of desire and denial. A week spent on camera might just turn Lucy and Seb's relationship from family-friendly to *viewer discretion advised…*

PRAISE FOR OLIVIA DADE

With richly drawn characters you'll love to root for, Olivia Dade's books are a gem of the genre—full of humor, heart, and heat.

KATE CLAYBORN

[*Teach Me*] made me cry at my desk at work (a true badge of honor). Dade's slow-burn romance follows ice queen history teacher Rose and her new co-worker, Martin, over the course of a school year, and it made me want to call and thank all the kind teachers I ever had. Rose and Martin are good, complicated, devoted people, and the way they pine for each other is rendered by Dade in all its aching beauty.

BOOKPAGE, STARRED REVIEW

[W]hen a work comes along that feels entirely new in all the best ways, I tend to take notice. As I read Olivia Dade's newest, *Teach Me*, I felt just that. ... I adored *Teach Me* from top to bottom and I'm sure it'll be on my best of list come December. Thanks for this one, Ms. Dade.

ALL ABOUT ROMANCE, DESERT ISLE KEEPER REVIEW

Believing matters. So to all my readers: Thank you for believing in me.

PROLOGUE

Cowan paused the video footage on his monitor—small, as befitted a lowly intern at the Home and Away Television Network—and turned to Irene. "This dude's definitely a serial killer."

She glanced up from her tablet, where she'd been answering texts and messages from various HATV staff. "He looks normal enough to me."

As he'd discovered over the past weeks, her standards for applicants to Tiny House Trackers were simultaneously more and less stringent than this. When they screened submissions, she weeded out anyone she considered boring, even people he considered acceptable options. Accountants, data entry clerks, lawyers: all dismissed with a flick of her wrist.

Potential murderers, however, did not appear to constitute a problem for her.

"He was very insistent that his tiny house have large storage areas with sturdy locks on the outside and no knobs on the inside. Also room on the walls for his meat hooks." Cowan shuddered. "God help any census taker who stops by during fava bean season."

She didn't look convinced. "Maybe he hunts wild boar or sasquatches or something."

"Sasquatches don't exist."

"I'm a city girl." She shrugged. "All wildlife seems mythical and exotic to me."

"I don't think the greater ease of Sasquatch hunting is the reason he wants to live alone in the woods." He leaned forward, ready to click to the next interview. "As far as I'm concerned, he's a no."

Her stylus tapped against the edge of her tablet as she considered the matter. "Not so fast. Featuring him might help goose our ratings. Maybe we could even propose filming a follow-up special, *Tiny House of Terror*."

She might have begun her internship with HATV only a few months before him, but that time had clearly jaded her.

"Forget it." He typed NO into his applicant spreadsheet, letting the rare all-caps refusal express his strong feelings on the matter. "I'm not going to be responsible for any tiny house carnage."

"Suit yourself." She turned back to her messages. "But don't blame me when we end up featuring yet another cash-strapped single with four enormous dogs who wants full-size appliances, a bathtub, and a king bed in less than a hundred square feet for a budget of about twenty bucks."

He cringed at the mere thought of it.

Right now, the two of them were sitting in a forgotten corner of the HATV studios, occupying a room of approximately that same size. Only a couple of chipped desks, two computers, and stained tan carpeting filled the space. Yet even without a single refrigerator, bathtub, or mattress, the force of Irene's presence made the room feel tight.

He couldn't imagine trying to fit an entire household into such a tiny footprint. But that's what people had been clamoring to do, and they wanted to broadcast their tiny house search via HATV. Which meant interns like he and Irene spent way too many hours sorting through applicants.

With a sigh, he clicked on the next possibility, a thirty-something woman named Lucy Finch. "Better a boring participant than someone who hunts villagers for sport."

She snorted. "After another month of this, you'll think differently. Trust me."

When Lucy Finch filled his monitor, he groaned. "Oh, Jesus. Another latter-day hippie type."

"Told you," Irene said.

He began to take stock of the woman. White. Blond hair. Brown eyes. Tortoise-shell frames for her glasses. Long, frizzy curls that tangled with her dangling peace-sign earrings. No makeup. A nose stud and a wide, tentative smile. Some kind of flowy tie-dyed top, and if he wasn't mistaken...

He looked closer, squinting as she wiggled in the chair to get herself settled.

Yup. No bra. Certain viewers would definitely appreciate *that*.

"Tell us about yourself," urged Martha, the woman who conducted all the interviews for Tiny House Trackers. "Your name, your job, and why you need a tiny house."

"I'm Lucy Finch." The woman was fiddling with something in her palm, rubbing her thumb in circles against it again and again. "I'm a licensed and Board-Certified massage therapist in Marysburg, Virginia. I used to manage our local Massage Mania, but I was just promoted. Now I'm going to help open new locations around the country and train their managers and employees."

It seemed Ms. Finch possessed a certain amount of professional ambition, which he duly noted in his spreadsheet.

With her free hand, she tucked a hank of curls behind her ear. "I'll be moving frequently. I decided living in a tiny house that could move with me made more sense than month-by-month rentals or hotel rooms. And I liked the idea of paring my belongings down to the minimum and leaving a smaller carbon footprint."

"Why did you choose to apply to Tiny House Trackers?" Martha's warm voice came from behind the camera. "What factors played into your decision?"

The woman winced. "Well, to be honest, it wasn't really my idea. My friend Allie convinced me."

A rustling of papers offscreen. "And Allie is your real estate agent?"

"She said she could find me a great tiny house in the area. I'm not quite sure what I want yet, but—"

"A yurt." Irene was still perusing her tablet. "That type always goes for a yurt."

"You don't know that." He gestured to the monitor. "She might choose a cabin in a forest where she can hug trees whenever she wants. Or a converted train car that she'll paint with peace symbols and decorate with tie-dyed scarves and posters of Jerry Garcia. There are lots of possibilities."

"Mark my words. There are yurt people and non-yurt people, and trust me, kid, she's a yurt person."

He folded his arms across his chest. "I'm actually older than you."

"Maybe in years. Not in wisdom."

Lucy Finch was still talking. "—room to store my massage table when I'm not using it, in case I see clients on the side. A bathroom big enough for those clients to change. If I have a loft, steps instead of a ladder, so my dog can—"

Blah, blah, blah. Sweet smile and braless state notwithstanding, her story wouldn't grab viewer attention, not enough for their ratings to draw even with their competitor's tiny house show, and she didn't seem like the type to break down or throw a fit on camera. Not good fodder for unscripted television.

He made a few more notes in the spreadsheet and prepared to reject yet another potential participant. Dammit, Irene had a point when it came to Mr. Silence of the Tiny House Lambs. Maybe they could conduct a poll during the episode about whether the man hunted wildlife or hapless tourists, and even add a few tips in a chyron about how to escape from backwoods cabins of horror.

Martha was wrapping up her questions. "Would you want to include a friend or significant other in your tiny house search?"

Poised to click to the next interview, his hand stilled on the mouse.

With that question, Ms. Finch's whole demeanor had changed. Her smile spread to her eyes, which crinkled appealingly behind her glasses. Her thumb slowed its circles, then stopped altogether. Her shoulders lowered, and she sat back in her chair.

"If you chose me as a participant, my friend Sebastián Castillo would accompany me." She laughed, the sound warm and low. "Much to his dismay."

"He doesn't want to help you?" Martha's voice had sharpened, but not with impatience. With interest, as she sensed the same shift Cowan had.

"He likes to keep a low profile. He'd rather break a limb than be on television." She wrinkled her nose. "I felt terrible about asking him, but I need his support and input. I trust him more than anyone else I know. And when I offered to bother someone else, he said that wasn't necessary."

Beside Cowan, Irene had raised her head to watch Ms. Finch. "Huh."

"How long have you and Sebastián known one another?" Martha asked.

"Since high school. His family moved from California to live closer to relatives in the D.C. area, and we became friends almost immediately. Even after graduation, we stayed in touch through letters and phone calls, and we saw each other whenever he came to visit his parents. When he moved back to Marysburg last year, we became close again."

She'd set aside the object in her palm, placing it on a nearby table. A rock, he now saw. A worry stone. And as she talked about Sebastián, she gestured with both hands, her face lit with enthusiasm.

"Have you two ever dated?"

"No." Ms. Finch paused, and her smile turned wistful. "No. Although I always wond—" She cut herself off. "No, we haven't."

"Would Mr. Castillo's spouse object to his assisting you? Or a significant other of some sort?"

Clever Martha. Cutting to the heart of the matter in the guise of professional concern.

"He's not dating anyone right now." Ms. Finch bit her lip. "He broke up with his last girlfriend shortly after I moved to Marysburg."

"I just bet he did." Irene had shoved her tablet to one side and was drumming her fingers on the desk, as she always did when excited. "Cowan, switch to his interview."

Lucy Finch's brows had drawn together. "But I don't want to give you the wrong impression. Our relationship has never been romantic in any—"

Sebastián Castillo's face replaced his longtime friend's on the monitor.

Golden-brown skin. Black hair, short along the sides, longer and a bit choppy on top. Either dark brown or black eyes. Thick brows. Clean-shaven. A crisp button-down shirt, his tie slightly loosened and askew.

Unlike Ms. Finch, he didn't bother to force a smile. He

wasn't frowning, either, though. Instead, his face revealed nothing. No nervousness. No impatience. No emotion whatsoever. His expression was as smooth as Ms. Finch's worry stone.

It remained so as he answered Martha's initial question.

His hands lay flat on the table before him. "I'm thirty-three. A mechanical engineer. I help my company modify our engine designs to meet upcoming emissions legislation."

Martha didn't waste any more time on irrelevant topics. "And why did you agree to help Lucy with her tiny house search?"

Irene had leaned forward, her green eyes sharp on Mr. Castillo's face.

Cowan returned his attention to the interview just in time to see the transformation.

Sebastián Castillo's stony façade cracked at the mere mention of Lucy Finch's name. His countenance softened, his fingers curled into loose fists, and the corners of his mouth tucked inward. An abortive smile? A frown of worry? Cowan couldn't tell, but it was something. Something that might make for very, very good television.

"She needs me." That was all Mr. Castillo said. For him, it was clearly enough.

"And you'd do anything for her?" Martha prodded.

At that, an almost indecipherable smile stretched his lips, affectionate and a touch sad. "Anything. Even go on a cable reality show."

Irene whistled. "He's hot as hell when he smiles."

Cowan let out his own slow breath as he battled irrational annoyance. "He's also half in love with Lucy Finch, unless I miss my guess."

"I think the feeling's mutual." Her head tilted, and her fingers resumed drumming against the table. "Although I suppose they could just be really good friends and nothing more."

"Maybe." With reluctance, he pointed out the obvious. "She's about to buy a yurt and move away from him."

His coworker reached for her tablet and opened a new document. "Maybe that'll depend on how the tiny house hunt goes."

He slanted her a warning look. "We can't sabotage the houses she sees."

"That's correct. But my guess is that the options are limited in her corner of Virginia." Irene's gamine face, so familiar after weeks of working side by side, stretched into a grin. "And we don't have to help her real estate agent find better ones. We can also give a heads-up to the crew."

Any certainty he'd briefly possessed was crumbling into doubt. "I'm not sure we should mess with people's lives for the sake of good TV."

"We aren't doing it for the sake of good TV. It's more of a humanitarian mission than anything else. A good deed." A gleaming swath of jet-black hair swung in front of her face, hiding her expression. "Aren't Boy Scouts like you supposed to like good deeds?"

His head gave a warning twinge, as it often did when Irene got that particular tone.

"I don't know. It still seems a bit...manipulative, I guess. And I wasn't a Boy Scout." He hesitated, then amended, "Not for long, anyway."

She snickered. "Nailed it."

"Irene..." He scrubbed his face with both hands.

"Trust me."

He didn't. But he also didn't object when she sent a quick note to their boss.

I think we have our next episode. Suggestions for the crew forthcoming.

ONE

Coffee. Sebastián needed coffee. Preferably in IV form, administered stat.

An entire week loomed ahead of him, full of cameras and microphones and intrusive questions and strangers and too-tight spaces. Full of Lucy and the prospect of her imminent departure.

Not since high school had he confronted such an exciting array of horrors, and he hadn't missed that tug of dread deep in his gut. It was a familiar but unwelcome companion, dragging him by the hand into shadows.

So yeah, if he didn't plan to break his promise to his best friend—and he wouldn't, although he knew she would react to his about-face with her usual easygoing acceptance—he could at least ensure he remained adequately caffeinated, despite his pre-dawn awakening and early arrival at work. Despite the entire day of—God help him—filming that awaited him.

His fellow early-bird coworkers had gathered around the employer-provided gourmet coffee machine, their version of an old-school water cooler. But he didn't have any choice in the matter. He couldn't wait them out, not this morning.

They moved aside so he could reach the machine, and their conversation—something about sacks and yardage—continued while he filled his stainless-steel mug.

Only Gwen greeted him with a nod, her silver-streaked ponytail swinging. "Morning."

She still hadn't given up on him, even after a year. Nice lady, but entirely too persistent.

"Morning." He nodded to her and swiveled toward the mini-refrigerator. Just a splash of milk, and he'd be—

"We were just talking about the game last night. Are you a football fan, Sebastián?"

At her question, all the other engineers turned to him, and he paused.

Football didn't interest him. Fútbol was more his speed. But they didn't need to know that. If he told them, maybe they'd make a snide comment about how much "foreigners" loved soccer, and maybe they wouldn't.

To be fair, they probably wouldn't.

He still wasn't willing to risk it.

"Sure," he said, pouring the milk carefully into his mug.

Bill, the resident expert on all things sports-related, brightened. "Any particular team? The Rams? The Raiders?"

Sebastián never should have told them he'd moved from California, but how could he avoid a direct question without damaging his already-tenuous relationships with his colleagues? And how could he get out of this conversation with speed but without outright rudeness?

"They're all great." A quick sip from his mug established that he'd added enough milk. "Listen, I need to get going. I'm leaving work early today, and I have a few projects to complete before then. Have a good day, everyone."

A forced smile, this one directed at the whole group, before he made his escape.

One obstacle down. But compared to what lay ahead of him, an entire day of public exposure and claustrophobic rooms and Lucy, the conversation at the water cooler was nothing. He'd need to keep a tight lid on himself. More so than usual, even.

At his desk, he put in his earbuds and started a MATLAB simulation running. And when Gwen called across the room and asked him where he was going later that day, he pretended not to hear.

"This cozy cabin is one hundred and twenty square feet, has one sleeping loft, and comes in ten thousand dollars below the top end of your budget." Allie gestured toward the dilapidated wooden shack nestled among the trees. "I think it's a great option for you."

Lucy pursed her lips, attempting not to laugh on camera. *Cozy* was clearly real-estate-agent code for *ridiculously small*.

Sebastián said nothing, just studied the structure in silence. Then again, Lucy hadn't expected him to express his opinion without prompting. After all these years, he was unlikely to change his communication style, whether or not cameras and a boom mic hovered nearby.

"What are your first impressions?" Allie asked.

Lucy searched for a diplomatic answer. "I love the setting. Very tranquil."

Sure, she wouldn't actually live in this area much longer, and the house didn't come with the property. But maybe viewers wouldn't remember that.

"You won't leave much of a carbon footprint with this

option." Allie's smile seemed brighter than normal. Wider too. "And what an opportunity to make this place your own with a few minor updates!"

More code. By *a few minor updates*, Lucy assumed Allie meant *extensive renovations to keep your flimsy new home from collapsing under the weight of an errant chipmunk*.

Allie rapped on a piece of dry, cracked siding with her knuckles. Then, when it creaked ominously at the contact, she snatched her hand away. "Just look at the lovely natural patina of this wood."

Ah, yes. Patina. Also known as dry rot.

Ostensibly, Allie was talking to her, but Lucy's friend and real estate agent kept both eyes on the camera at all times. And during each break in filming, she didn't hang out with Lucy and Sebastián. Not even to tell them one of her notoriously dirty jokes or share recent pictures of her kids. Instead, she kept company with the crew, asking them questions and dropping tidbits from her own résumé.

For years, Allie had talked about leaving what she considered the stifling confines of Marysburg, not to mention the orbit of her feckless ex-husband. Lucy just hadn't realized the search for a tiny house was meant to serve as her friend's exit plan. She should have, though, when Allie had pushed her to apply for Tiny House Trackers.

And really, Allie *should* grasp this opportunity. Her friend deserved the future of her dreams. If Lucy had hoped for a bit more support during this process, that was a problem with her, not Allie. This was, it seemed, yet another occasion in which Jarrod's complaints about Lucy's naïveté had proven correct.

Even two months after their breakup, she could still hear his voice. His disdain.

She slipped her hand into the pocket of her skirt. Her worry stone—amethyst for calm—slid into her palm, a welcome and familiar weight. She rubbed her thumb against the smooth, cool surface as she contemplated her first tiny house possibility.

She turned to Sebastián. "What do you think?"

"What I think isn't important." He stepped closer to her, his black hair shining almost blue in the dappled forest sunlight. "This experience is all about you. So what are your initial thoughts?"

She bit her lip. "I'd hoped it would be a bit bigger."

At least two hundred square feet, as she'd told Allie. Big enough for Hairy Garcia, her energetic golden retriever. Big enough to have room for her massage table.

"Well, you wanted a tiny house!" Allie laughed, but her eyes narrowed in warning. "You need to be realistic, Lucy."

A comment she'd heard before, too many times. Lucy studied the leaves underfoot, her thumb circling and circling.

"I believe she asked for at least two hundred square feet." Sebastián widened his stance, his right eyebrow cocked. "This is significantly smaller than that."

Her shoulders unknotted, and she let out a slow breath of relief. Yes. Yes, that was exactly what she'd have said to Allie, if only she'd had enough confidence in her own position.

Typical Sebastián: always on her side, always her champion. From the very beginning.

Ever since he'd transferred to Marysburg High as a junior, he'd defended her from anything that might hurt her, even while he'd fended off countless bullies of his own. Too many of their classmates had proven eager to hassle the new kid in school, a Guatemalan-American boy who hadn't grown tall or strong until well after graduation. A boy who refused to cower or back down no matter what was said or done to him. A boy who gradually shut off all visible emotional reactions to make himself an unsatisfying target for his persecutors.

A boy who became her best and most faithful friend.

Her battles, her wounds, had not been nearly as vicious or bloody as his. Still, he'd tried to protect her to the best of his ability. He might not have ever expressed his affection for her in words—she suspected he might not even be *able* to do so, not anymore—but he'd demonstrated that affection so many times she couldn't doubt it.

Behind a fold of her skirts, where the camera couldn't see the gesture, she took his hand in hers. It was broad and warm and strong now, vital and electric. A man's hand, not a boy's. But it was still the hand of the best champion an easily hurt teenage girl could have had. She gave his fingers a squeeze of gratitude, and then let him go, before someone could draw the wrong conclusion about them.

Someone like her, for example.

She'd always thought that someday, maybe...

But it wasn't going to happen. Not now, as she prepared to move halfway across the country. No matter how enticing he appeared in that formfitting Henley and those well-worn jeans. No matter how soft and warm his eyes became when he looked at her. No matter how her fingers tingled when they touched.

The camerawoman moved closer to Allie, capturing her tight smile in response to Sebastián's matter-of-fact challenge.

"Yes, Lucy wanted a slightly bigger house. But the supply of tiny houses in this area of Virginia is limited, as you know. That said, I'm sure we'll find a great option among the choices I've located. Lucy just needs to be flexible." Allie headed for the door, which rose high above the forest floor because of the trailer beneath the house. "Let's go inside."

Lucy let Allie and the crew precede her. Sebastián stayed by her side, as she'd anticipated.

Unsure of the boom mic's range, she spoke in a whisper.

"I'm concerned about the condition of the house. It seems more weathered than I'd hoped. And I think it's too small for my needs, although the inside could be very charming." She paused. "In a hobbit-enthusiast sort of way. I hadn't pictured living on the wrong side of the tracks in the Shire."

He closed his eyes and bowed his head, the telltale sign he was fighting a smile.

"Come on. Spill it." She poked his arm with her free hand, startled as always by the feel of firm muscle beneath her fingertip. The foreign, enticing hardness made her want to linger, to slide her fingertips up over his shoulders and down that straight, strong back of his. Instead, she dropped her hand to her side. "Tell me what you're thinking."

When he raised his face, a small smile had cracked his stoic features. "I wonder whether the price includes cookie-making elves."

She giggled and deposited the worry stone back in her pocket. "I'm pretty sure Allie would have mentioned that."

"I hope she forgot. Because this place should definitely contain a tiny elven fudge-filled-cookie factory, given the asking price and the condition." Arms akimbo, he stared up at the cabin, his grin fading. "If it doesn't, I'd hesitate before buying."

"At least it's towable, once I get a truck." She peered at the trailer beneath the house. "Since it's approximately the size of my childhood dollhouse."

A shallow furrow in his brow appeared for a split second. "Before we go inside, I need to know more about what you want. Just how soon do you need a house? How far will you have to tow it? And how often do you think you'll move?"

They should have discussed the logistics of her move weeks earlier, of course, but they hadn't. On her side, because the prospect of leaving Marysburg seemed much more fraught, much more painful, when Seb was within touching distance. On his side...

Well, her friend didn't ask many personal questions. Not of her. Not of anyone.

"I'm taking a few weeks of vacation to travel around the country before my new job starts, so I have a little time, but not much. And I might move...I don't know. Twice a year, maybe?" She hadn't asked for many details before accepting the job. The gut-level imperative to escape had driven the decision, as well as her hope that a fresh start would silence the critical voices Jarrod had left in her head. "My first assignment is in Minneapolis, like I told you, but after that they can send me anywhere across the country."

He fell silent for a minute before responding, his voice neutral. "Minneapolis is a long way from here."

It felt longer as each day passed and her departure from her hometown, from her clients, from her circle of female friends, and—most of all—from Sebastián became imminent.

"Don't worry." She forced a smile. "I'll write you a couple times a week, just like I always did."

He shifted his shoulders. "I'll write back."

"Just like *you* always did." She forced a smile. "With admirable promptness."

But he'd never initiated contact himself. Instead, he'd let her take the lead, just as he'd done since high school. If she ever stopped writing or calling him, stopped asking him to her house or inviting herself to his, she suspected she'd never hear from him again.

He wasn't capable of more, which was why she'd never asked for more. But what he gave her was more than enough to make him a treasured friend. One she'd miss terribly when she left Marysburg.

She knew she was important to him, even though he'd never said it.

Except maybe once, in that graduation limerick.

"Depending on where you're assigned, you might end up in vastly different climates," he said. "You'll need something sturdy, with good heating, cooling, and weather-proofing."

"And this Smurf mansion isn't it."

"Is that what you think?"

He wouldn't make the decision for her, which was both frustrating and flattering. He trusted her judgment. Now she needed to do the same.

She nodded. "Yes. I'm happy to tour the inside of the place, though. For the sake of good TV, if nothing else."

As if on cue, the producer poked her head out of the cabin door. To her credit, Jill didn't appear impatient. Instead, she grinned at the two of them with seemingly genuine warmth. "Come on up, slowpokes. And a quick reminder: Try not to speak outside the range of the mic, if at all possible. We want as much usable footage as we can get."

Jill had explained earlier that as a relatively new and low-budget show, Tiny House Trackers used a small crew, so Lucy and Seb needed to stay near the two cameras and the mic. Unlike a few other shows on the network, there was no script either. HATV was attempting to keep the television experience authentic. Lucy truly hadn't visited any of the houses before, much less bought one already, and in the end, she could either pick one of the three options or choose to keep looking.

Given what she'd seen from Allie so far, Lucy suspected the latter choice would cost her a friend. And although she had plenty of those, including several true sisters of her heart, she hated to alienate anyone.

Especially Allie, her childhood neighbor. The girl who'd told scary stories in front of backyard campfires and inside tents, a flashlight beneath her chin as she wailed like a ghost. The girl who'd insisted on playing Light as a Feather, Stiff as a Board during every sleepover and always spread her sleeping bag beside Lucy's. The girl who'd been part of every birthday celebration, every block party, and every camping trip Lucy's parents had planned.

The last traces of that girl had disappeared years ago, around the time of Allie's divorce, and Lucy understood why. She'd always hoped the friend she'd once known might return to her someday, though.

She was beginning to suspect that wouldn't happen. But it didn't matter, not now. Not when Allie, a camera crew, and Sebastián were all waiting for her to tour the inside of a dilapidated shack and pronounce it fit for human—or elven—habitation.

"I guess I can't put it off any longer," she muttered. "Where are my glasses?"

Sebastián produced them from his pocket. "You left them on the craft services table. You took them off to read the ingredient lists."

"Well, that explains why the house seems kind of fuzzy, as well as tiny." She accepted the glasses and settled them on her nose. "Never mind. The house *is* fuzzy."

"Moss and mold."

She sighed. "Moss and mold on the places that don't have dry rot instead. Lovely."

"Speaking of which..." Sebastián's features had settled back into inscrutability. "Be careful on the steps."

A flimsy set of mildewing plastic steps stood before the cabin entrance. Sebastián ignored them, bounding up into the doorway with a single, athletic leap. But since she was wearing a long, full skirt, rather than pants, and couldn't boast his six feet of height, those gray-tinged steps would have to suffice for her.

He held her arm as she climbed them, not leaving the

doorway until she stood on solid ground once more. Then, in unison, they shifted to look at the inside of the cabin.

No. No, no, no, no.

The words emerged before Lucy could bite her tongue. "Holy shit."

"Cut," called Jill.

TWO

"So the guy who's selling this place..." Lucy's eyes flicked to the side as she searched for the right words. "Is he still, um, around?"

Allie's blond brows drew together. "Are you asking whether he's dead?"

Lucy gestured toward the hydroponics setup that dominated the minuscule kitchen. Or, more accurately, toward the flourishing marijuana plants growing in that setup. "No. More whether he's in jail. Because if he isn't already, he will be once this episode airs."

Jill waved a hand. "According to my notes, he's hiking the Appalachian Trail. Don't worry, we'll cut out anything that would put him in legal jeopardy."

"Oh, good." Lucy's lips quirked. "What are you going to use as this house's nickname for the show? The Weed-Grower's Way-Station? Mary Jane's Manor? The Dank Dasha?"

The cameraman snickered, amused. Sebastián couldn't blame him. As naïve and innocent as Lucy seemed, she had a sneaky sense of humor. One he'd appreciated for well over a decade now.

"The Adventurer's Abode." Jill grinned. "It seemed fitting and less likely to get anyone arrested."

"Nice alliteration." With a couple of steps, Lucy bypassed the kitchen—which, he noted, boasted only a dorm-size refrigerator and a hot plate for her cooking convenience—and headed toward the area underneath the loft. Then she stopped again, this time beside a rough hole sawed into a built-in bench.

The two cameras began filming once more, and the sound guy positioned the boom mic overhead, just in time to catch her hushed question.

"Is this..." She paused, then tried again. "Is this...the facilities?"

Allie strode into camera view and positioned herself by the hole. "It's a wonderful feature, isn't it? This setup uses so much less water than a traditional toilet. And I know how badly you want to lessen your carbon footprint."

"It's a hole in a bench." Bending from the waist, Lucy peered inside the hole, careful not to let her long hair drop into the void. "With a plastic bag inside. One which, thankfully, appears unused. And there's no door separating it from the rest of the house."

"So environmentally responsible and personally liberating." Allie smoothed her own hair. "It's a real selling point. We're fortunate someone hasn't snapped up this property already."

The woman had no shame. Sebastián could have told Lucy that back in high school, but she wouldn't have believed him. She was, always and forever, determined to believe the best of everyone. Luckily, most of her friends had justified her continued loyalty.

Allie, not so much. And he had the feeling, from the stricken looks Lucy occasionally directed her old friend's way, that she was starting to realize it.

"Allie," Lucy whispered. "Could we talk for a minute without cameras?"

Her ostensible friend ignored the request, turned to the nearest camera, and began enumerating the very limited charms of the rundown shack in a determinedly cheerful tone.

Lucy's head dropped to her chest, and she stood silent and still for a minute.

Sebastián fisted his hands in his pockets.

Over the years, he'd tamed his out-of-control emotions. Very little bothered him. He knew he was a good son, a good brother, and a good friend. Handsome enough not to lack for female company when he desired it. Smart enough to succeed in his chosen field. Strong enough to defend himself if necessary. No insult imaginable could shake his confidence or provoke a reaction, and except around his family, he chose to keep any inconvenient feelings tucked safely away from view.

But Lucy's wounded expression gutted him. Always had.

It didn't matter whether the person who hurt her was a stranger, a friend like Allie, or an ex-boyfriend like that jackass Jarrod. Either way, Sebastián wanted to rage on her behalf. To demand apologies and offer them to her as her due. To comfort her by any means necessary.

But she was leaving. And although she'd no doubt send letters and postcards and e-mail messages, as she'd done until he'd returned to Marysburg last year, soon he wouldn't be able to protect her or bask in her sunny presence any longer.

When she left this time, he knew she wouldn't come back, to Marysburg or to him, and that knowledge had honed an unwelcome edge of desperation inside him. Still, if buying a tiny house and moving away would restore her faith in herself, would bring back her sparkle, he'd do whatever it took to support her efforts.

Even if her imminent departure felt like suffocating slowly in a dark, airless room.

After depositing her worry stone in her pocket, Lucy squared her shoulders and finally responded to Allie. "I appreciate the environmentalism of the facilities, but I'm not sure my level of personal liberation is sufficient for the task of using them." She winced. "I'm sorry. I may not believe in bras or leg-shaving, but apparently I draw the line at open-air toilets."

When Allie heaved an aggrieved sigh, he managed to keep his mouth shut.

Off-camera, the producer was waving them toward the loft. The only problem: Sebastián wasn't certain Lucy could even get into it, at least not while wearing a long skirt.

"I'm sure you're excited by the innovative loft access design." Allie looked at the wall to the left of the loft. "I'll let you explore that area without me. I'd just be in the way."

Translation: She didn't think she could get up there either.

"It's a rock-climbing wall." With an audible swallow, Lucy reached out to touch one of the fake stones anchored into the wood paneling. "There's no ladder to the loft? Or steps?"

"Nope." Allie bounded down the steps and disappeared outside.

Lucy cast a look of appeal at Jill. "If I'm climbing up there in a skirt, I really don't want to be filmed while doing so."

"Fair enough." Jill nodded to the crew, who put down their cameras and mic. "Why don't you two check out the loft together? Really take your time and see how you feel about such a small space, Lucy. And Sebastián, it's so fortunate you're here. She'll be able to figure out how things would work if she had company."

He instinctively swallowed a howl of protest.

What the hell was wrong with him? Why couldn't he

simply accept that his old friend was starting a new life without him? One where she might have another man in her bed?

"We'll join you two in a minute." Jill headed outside too, followed by the rest of the crew.

Suddenly, he and Lucy were alone. She met his gaze with a smile, but that worry stone was in her palm again, and her soft brown eyes were anxious.

"Why don't I climb up to the loft first?" He tested the holds and found them strong enough to support either of them, which came as a pleasant surprise. "Then I can help you, if you need it."

To his relief, she laughed. "Oh, I'll need it. We both know that."

Halfway up the wall, he got his first real glimpse of the space into which he and Lucy were supposed to squeeze. Pausing for a moment, he took a slow, deep breath.

"Allie called it a cozy nest built for two." Her tone was wry. "I'm guessing that means it's essentially a double-wide coffin."

He swallowed. "You're not wrong."

For Lucy, he could do this. For her, he'd do anything.

"Here goes nothing," he said.

Within a moment, he'd made it to the top of the wall and levered himself over the side of the loft. He couldn't sit up straight, not even in the center, where the pitched roof was highest.

"How is it up there?" She sounded tentative but curious.

It was dark. Too warm. The walls pressed in on him.

My breathing. I need to control my breathing. Slow, deep breaths. In. Out. In. Out.

He couldn't panic. Lucy needed him.

Rolling onto his stomach, he scooted his upper body over the edge of the loft and reached out with both hands toward the rock wall. "Make sure your skirt doesn't catch in your feet as you climb. And grab onto my hands if you feel unsteady." His fingers were damp and trembling, and he wiped them on his jeans before extending them once more. "You can do it."

She reached down and drew the back hem of her skirt up between her thighs, tucking it into the elastic waistband at the front. "Voila. Problem solved."

Gazing at her bare legs, as it turned out, proved an effective distraction from his discomfort. Long and curvy, they were pale from the skirts she always wore. He hadn't seen those legs uncovered since…when? That pool party the senior year of high school?

He'd only gone because she'd asked. He'd known how some of the other kids would respond to his skinny, hairless chest and the other obvious signs of his nonexistent puberty. Sure enough, before the end of the night, she'd wound up standing between him and a sophomore attempting to pick a fight, no matter how hard he'd tried to move Lucy and how often he'd told her it didn't matter, the insults didn't bother him, he'd simply walk away.

The asshole had accidentally punched her in the mouth while aiming for Sebastián. And the next thing Sebastián remembered, both he and that kid had been sprawled across the concrete, throwing fists and elbows and trying to inflict maximum damage on each other.

After that incident, everyone had known the simple truth: He wasn't impenetrable. He had a weakness. He cared about something, which meant it—she—could be used to hurt him. For those last few weeks of school, he'd waded into losing fight after losing fight in her defense, whenever other boys had insulted her or talked about her in gross, sexual terms in his presence.

He hadn't wanted her that way. He hadn't wanted *anyone*

that way, not then. But the denigration of the best, purest thing that had ever happened to him, the way they'd tried to demean her and talked about her with such greasy familiarity, had stripped reason from him.

Thank God for graduation. Without it, he might have either been expelled or permanently injured.

Now he could appreciate the view in a way that would never have occurred to him in high school. And those legs were worth the wait, by God. They weren't model-slim. They weren't even smooth, thanks to her hippie-girl defiance of female beauty norms.

But they were strong and curvaceous and…hers.

They were hers. And that was enough to vanquish his defenses.

"Sebastián? Are you okay?"

Somehow, she'd climbed up the wall without him noticing, and now she was reaching for his hands to steady herself as she transferred to the loft. When her fingers intertwined with his, warm and agile, he had to beat back a sudden, unexpected wave of heat.

"I've got you," he said.

Then she was tumbling on top of him, and it was completely awkward and wrong and painful. She was lying face-down on his back, her head near his legs. His neck bent at an uncomfortable angle under her weight, and her elbow poked into his thigh as she lifted her upper body.

He barely registered the pain as—for a millisecond only—the back of his head pressed up against a place he'd never allowed himself to imagine. At least, not outside of dreams he'd tried his best to forget.

In those dreams, that place hadn't been resting on the back of his head or covered by voluminous layers of skirts. No, he'd had it bare and spread before him like a feast.

Don't think about it. This is not what you and Lucy are about.

She was wiggling and squirming to turn around in the small space, and Christ, she smelled good. Like honey and musk. Then they were both on their backs and she was resting beside him. He missed her warm weight atop him. But she was still snuggled to his side in the center of the loft, since the edges wouldn't fit any normal human.

Her breast, small and soft, pressed against his left arm, and his body reacted in a very unwelcome way.

He pictured the Marysburg stream, his go-to calming image for over fifteen years now. The one he called to mind whenever he needed to quash an unwanted emotional or physical reaction. The spot where he and Lucy had spent so many peaceful afternoons after the last bell, reading and talking in the grass as they soaked their feet in the clear, cool water.

That image had saved him from disgrace and embarrassment more times than he could count, but he'd never told her. How could he, without exposing everything he'd tried so hard to hide?

"Wow." She wriggled again, and the image wasn't working anymore. Because it too was full of Lucy, her smile and soft skin and laughter and ineffable presence. Her bare legs and honeyed scent. "This is even tighter than I'd imagined."

Oh, Jesus.

With an effort, he kept his voice casual. "Welcome to Concussion Alley."

"Goddess help you if you sit up without thinking." She lifted her palm and pressed it against the ceiling. "I don't see how this is workable."

Voices drifted from below as the crew returned, and his heart rate began to slow. Surely these inappropriate reactions would cease once their private little bubble had been punctured?

The camerawoman called up, her voice damnably chipper. "We'll get set up in a minute. In the meantime, keep considering whether the space is big enough for two."

Lucy lowered her voice to a whisper. "I'm not even certain there's room for one person to lie on top of another."

No. No way. If this was going where he thought it was going—

Lucy touched his arm. "Can we test that, Seb?"

He lifted his head a bare inch and let it drop to the floor. Hard.

She cautiously raised herself on her elbow. "Are you okay? Did you hit your head?"

"I'm fine." He tried to unclench his teeth. "Are you sure you want to do this? I mean, with a camera crew nearby?"

In the dim light of the loft, he could see her small nod. "I need to find a house that will work for me. I think it would be a good thing to..." Her throat worked as she swallowed. "It would be a good thing to test."

She was definitely testing his resolve. He didn't know about anything else.

Compared to the mountains he'd move at her request, though, this was such a tiny appeal. And when would he get this chance ever again?

"Do you want me on top?" he asked. "Or beneath you?"

They were words he'd said many times before, in a completely different context.

Or maybe the context wasn't so different after all. Because when she breathed, "On top," his body reacted as if it were an invitation to bed her, and she was trembling as he moved over her and settled into the cradle of her body.

Then he could feel almost every inch of her beneath him, her warmth turning to heat as her lips parted and her breath caught. He stared down at that lush mouth of hers, wondering. Wanting. Waiting for her to stop him.

She didn't. And he couldn't remember anymore why this was a terrible idea.

Carefully, he cradled her head in his hand, while the other smoothed her tumbled hair back from her sweet, dazed face.

He had just enough mental capacity left to check. "Is this okay?"

She nodded, nibbling on her lower lip. In just a moment, he was going to take that lip into his own mouth and cherish it. Lick it in recompense for her abuse. Then maybe bite it again, but lightly. So lightly it would feel like a caress.

He lowered his head, and her eyes were heavy-lidded. Welcoming.

"So we've set up the shot from this angle—"

The camerawoman's voice, coming from only inches away, was a bucket of ice water poured over his body. He wrenched himself from Lucy, sitting up as quickly as he could.

That, as it turned out, was his next mistake.

THREE

"Are you sure you're okay?" As gently as she could, Lucy touched the lump on Sebastián's head. "I can drive us to an urgent care."

A rare tinge of grumpiness roughened his voice. "I'm fine. I just need a minute."

The producer had said HATV would cover any medical expenses, but Sebastián had refused treatment. "Stereotypical man," Jill had muttered to herself before leaving to discuss the situation with the crew.

Sebastián might have rebuffed the crew's fussing, but he'd let Lucy supervise his slow descent from the loft and guide him to a seat. She'd settled them both on the cramped, lumpy built-in couch—according to Allie, "the perfect loveseat in the perfect forest hideaway!"—while he recovered from the blow to his head. He'd never lost consciousness, his pupils seemed normal, and he remembered everything that had happened, so she was willing to let him decide how to treat the injury.

But jeez, he'd given himself quite a bump. At exactly the wrong moment, too. She'd almost thought…

Well, she'd surely been imagining things. He'd been helping her determine the loft's suitability for her future partners, nothing more. Another gallant gesture from a loyal friend.

His black hair had rumpled in all the hubbub, and she smoothed it into place. When he shifted his head away from her touch, she let her hand fall into her lap. Then into her pocket, where the worry stone waited, slick and cool and impervious to hurt.

"How's the patient doing?" Jill walked toward the couch, watching Sebastián with concern. "Did you change your mind about going to a doctor?"

"I'm fine," he repeated for the hundredth time. "But I do have a question. Where are the closets in here? Lucy's massage table needs a storage place."

Typical Sebastián, bringing the focus away from him and back to her needs.

Jill lifted a shoulder. "No need for closets. The guy who owns this house is a minimalist. Not to mention a naturist."

"He likes plants? I think we got that idea already, given the profusion of pot in the kitchen." Lucy tilted her head. "But what does that have to do with closets?"

Jill snorted. "A naturist isn't a plant lover."

"Then what is it?" Sebastián was rubbing his temples, but he stopped as soon as their attention turned to him.

"A nudist." Jill grinned at them. "The dude who owns this place is a nudist."

Lucy and Sebastián bolted up from the couch immediately.

A nudist elf. She was in the house of a nudist, weed-cultivating elf. And there weren't even any fudge-filled cookies or samples of edibles to be had.

"Those lumpy cushions…" She groaned. "Goddess help me, I don't want to know."

Sebastián was staring down at the couch, his lips pursed, but he didn't say a word.

"Sorry," Jill said. "I meant to warn you, but by the time I noticed you were sitting there, I figured the ball-sweat damage was already done."

Lucy sighed. "Let's disinfect our hands, and possibly the rest of our bodies and everything we've ever touched. Then why don't we find Sebastián a different, non-genitals-infused seat where he can rest while we finish filming?"

He shook his head gingerly. "Like I said, I'm okay. Let's get this done."

No argument she could muster would make him admit vulnerability, and she knew it. So she didn't argue, despite her worry. And luckily, the rest of the filming took less time than she'd imagined, given that the entire cabin could have fit inside her old condo's master bedroom. Everything went smoothly, up until the final conversation between her and Allie.

"So what's your overall impression?" her friend asked.

Lucy glanced at Sebastián, and his warm, dark gaze and little nod heartened her. She chose honesty. "I'm so sorry, Allie, but this place doesn't work for me. I need more space, and I need a house in better condition. I appreciate your showing it to me, though."

Allie gave a tiny sniff, her nostrils flaring. "For your budget, you can't afford everything you want. You may need to be more realistic about your tiny house expectations."

Sebastián shifted, clearly preparing to insert himself into the discussion, but Lucy lifted a hand, and he subsided.

She didn't want conflict. She just wanted this day to end. "Maybe so. Still, I'd like to see more options. I'm sure the next house will be perfect."

Allie offered the camera a gleaming smile. "It will be, or

my name isn't Allie Peachtree, Real Estate Queen of the Eastern Seaboard."

"Um..." Lucy blinked. She'd never heard anyone call Allie that before. Not once. Honestly, it didn't seem like the easiest name to remember. "Long may you reign?"

"Exactly." Allie descended the stairs and left without another word.

"That's a wrap for the day. See you tomorrow at eight o'clock sharp," Jill called out.

Thank goddess. Lucy couldn't wait to relax for the rest of the afternoon and evening. She grabbed her backpack and strode over to where Sebastián was staring up at the loft.

She poked him in the arm. "Picturing the various diseases we contracted while rolling around up here?"

Keep it light and breezy. Just because you misinterpreted what happened—in yet another spectacular display of poor judgment—doesn't mean you should make your friend uncomfortable.

"Yes." His eyes didn't meet hers, and she heard him swallow. "Yes, that's what I was picturing."

"Are you about to head home?" She jingled her keys. "Because after I stop at the hotel and take care of Hairy, I'm going to grab some dinner. I'd love for you to join me."

At that, he turned to her. "A hotel? Why aren't you and Hairy staying in your condo?"

"I moved out, as the Real Estate Queen of the Eastern Seaboard suggested." Nope. Still not rolling off the tongue. "She decided to stage the condo using nicer furniture than mine, so I had to move all my stuff into storage anyway. Then she asked me to keep it looking perfect until we got a good offer, and given how Hairy sheds, that didn't seem feasible if we stayed there. So I booked a pet-friendly hotel room with a good weekly rate. And since the condo sold so quickly and I'm leaving so soon on vacation, I didn't see the point of moving back in. Until I get my tiny house and transport it to Minneapolis, we're living out of a suitcase."

The corners of his mouth flicked downward, just for a second. "You didn't tell me you needed to move out so soon. I would have helped you get everything into storage."

She bit back her instinctive response: *You didn't ask.*

If she hadn't understood him so well, she'd have said he didn't care whether she stayed or went. But he did care. She knew he did. "No worries, Seb. I had lots of other friends to help me. If I'd been in a jam, I'd have called you, like I did with this house hunt."

Silence.

His jaw worked, and he shifted on his feet. But he didn't say anything, and she was too tired to wring more words or an answer to her dinner invitation out of him.

"I'll see you tomorrow morning, bright and early." She slung her backpack over her shoulder and found the key to her Prius. "Thank you again for helping me so much today. I owe you big."

Offering him a quick squeeze on his arm, she turned to go.

"You and Hairy shouldn't stay in a hotel and live out of a suitcase for weeks," he said, his voice low and gravelly. Hoarse, as if he'd had to wrest the words from his throat by force.

She slowly swiveled to face him, stunned into silence. The Sebastián she knew didn't tell her what she should and shouldn't do. He didn't contradict her decisions. Not ever.

"Seb..." What did he want from her? She didn't have any other good options. "It's fine. The hotel is decent, and everything we need is in my suitcase."

He shook his head, mouth tight. "I'm sure you picked a good place, but it's not as safe as a home, it's expensive, and it's not as comfortable for either of you. Stay with me instead."

Oh, he was such a good man. But for so many reasons, staying with him was a terrible idea. She'd managed to conjure a near-kiss from a friendly gesture today. Goddess only knew what sort of foolish conclusions she'd reach if they spent night after night in the same house.

"I can't impose on you or Kitty Hendrix like that. But I appreciate the offer." On impulse, she got up on tiptoe and kissed his smooth cheek. "The hotel will be fine. Don't worry about us."

He'd closed his eyes at the contact. "I…"

He struggled for words as she waited. Opened his eyes again. Curled his fingers into his palms, brow pinched.

"I want you to," he finally said. "I want you to stay with me. Otherwise, I'll worry."

Flabbergasted, she stared at him.

"Please." A vein in his temple throbbed, a telltale sign of his agitation. "Please, Lucy."

He'd never pleaded with her before. Not for anything. Not for comfort, or assistance, or even the television remote. So what, really, could she say to the man who'd been her faithful friend for over fifteen years?

"Okay." She swallowed hard. "Okay. If you're sure, we'll stay with you."

He let out a slow breath. "Good. Go get Hairy, and we'll meet at my house."

When he sprinted down the steps and out toward their cars, she was too confused to follow.

Self-contained, stoic Sebastián Castillo had just expressed what he wanted in words. Revealed a vulnerability. Admitted an emotion. What in the world was happening?

And did it mean she hadn't misinterpreted their encounter in the loft after all?

Hairy bounded through Sebastián's house the moment she let him off his leash, tail wagging as he barked with wholehearted enthusiasm. No doubt he'd detected the wonderful smells wafting from the kitchen. But Lucy knew her dog, and not even amazing food—had Seb made that delicious Guatemalan stew for her again?—could elicit this particular brand of fevered intensity.

No, Hairy had realized that Kitty Hendrix, his favorite friend in the whole wide world, was a mere room away, and he wanted to play with her. Now. Also for the rest of his life and well into any sort of doggie afterlife that might exist.

As she and Sebastián had discovered over the past year, that misguided enthusiasm wouldn't die, no matter how many times Kitty either regarded Hairy with bored, unmoving contempt or swiped at his nose with a disdainful paw.

Poor Kitty Hendrix was going to have a very exhausting couple of weeks. True, she was kind of an asshole. But Lucy still had a sneaking fondness for the cranky feline, probably because Sebastián had let her choose Kitty's name. He'd regretted that decision, of course, as soon as Lucy announced her pick, but by then it was too late. He was a man of his word.

A faint, surprised yelp echoed from one of the back rooms, and Lucy winced. Poor Hairy never seemed to remember how Kitty rewarded his fervent, lick-intensive greetings.

Sebastián wheeled Lucy's suitcase inside his house and locked the door behind them. "You'll stay in the master bedroom. I'll make some room for you in the closet and dresser, and there should be plenty of space to spread out in the bathroom. I've already changed the sheets and put out food and water for Hairy in the kitchen. Started some pepián for us too, since you must be tired of eating out."

So bossy. She couldn't get used to it, not after years of noncommittal responses and a seeming determination to let her guide the relationship at all times.

He wasn't using that bossiness against her or eyeing her with disdain, though. Wasn't telling her she'd made a foolish, unrealistic decision, or she expected too much, or apologized too often, or overtipped at dinner. Wasn't letting her know she was wrong, wrong, wrong, wrong. Always.

Goddess help her, Jarrod had started out so sweet. So supportive. At first, his corrections had seemed so minor, born out of his concern for her well-being. Over time, though, he'd become more critical, and she'd become less confident, and she'd nearly lost herself.

But Sebastián hadn't changed, not like Jarrod had. Her best friend didn't want to undermine her. He just wanted to protect and care for her, as he so often did. Only this time, he was willing to express that desire in words and take immediate action. All to meet her needs.

He didn't think she'd done anything wrong. He just wanted to cosset her. Feed her.

This type of bossiness didn't make her feel small. Instead, she felt…cherished.

It was delicious. She wanted more of it.

But that didn't mean she wouldn't put up an argument when necessary. "Thank you so much. I'd be fine in the guest room, though. Really."

"I turned the guest bedroom into a workout space." He began wheeling her suitcase down the hall. "It's either the master bedroom or my fold-out couch, and I'm not subjecting you to that."

She followed him, fascinated. Never before had she ventured this far into his home. Whenever she'd visited, he'd kept them safely ensconced in the public areas of the house. The kitchen, the den, the powder room. All nicely decorated, all generic. All revealing nothing important about the man who lived there.

"The couch will work," she said. "Please don't give up your own bedroom."

A token protest. She really wanted to see his damn room. To the point where if he didn't hurry up, she was going to shove ahead of him to get a peek.

"Your back is hurting." He swung open the door at the end of the hallway. "It's been hurting all day. If you sleep on that couch, you'll hobble for the next week."

Her jaw dropped. What else did Sebastián see but never discuss?

"You're walking like you do after too many two-hour massages, but it's probably from the moving instead." He heaved her suitcase onto a low wooden table. "Why don't you pour a drink and relax while I clear some space in the dresser?"

She hesitated. "Are you sure about my using this room? I don't want to inconvenience you more than absolutely necessary."

"I'm sure." He nodded toward the doorway. "You know how to use the television and DVR, so make yourself at home."

Oh, no. She wasn't leaving. Not when she had the chance to see him in his inner sanctum. His fortress of manly solitude. The place where he...

She looked around. Wow. The place where he didn't appear to do a hell of a lot, honestly. She'd expected it to be more personalized than the public spaces, but it wasn't. Other than a few photos of his family, most of which she'd seen displayed in his parents' house back in high school, the room was all dark wood and pale gray paint and comfortable-looking furniture.

No mementos on the dresser. No art on the walls. No magazines or books on the nightstand, even though she knew he loved to read.

Had he put his personal items away before her arrival? Or did his room always look this sterile?

A plaintive yowl drifted through the open doorway, and she winced. "Poor Kitty. She's probably getting licked to death."

"She'll be fine. Her standoffishness is mostly an act, anyway." He looked around the room. "Do you want Hairy with you here at night, or out in the living room?"

"The living room is perfect. He won't want to stray far from Kitty's side, anyway." She laughed. "She may never forgive you for this betrayal."

He shrugged. "She hasn't forgiven me for any number of other offenses either. I'll live."

"May I sit on the bed while you work?"

It stood in the center of the room, tall and wide and covered by a crisp, striped duvet. Two pillows encased in soft-looking charcoal-gray fabric lay in a precise row at the head of the mattress.

She wanted to jump on the bed and roll around. Tangle herself in the sheets and ruin that careful, pristine perfection. But she'd settle for sitting up against the solid, curved headboard and watching him go through a few of his drawers to make room for her.

He paused for a long moment, but he sounded unconcerned when he answered her. "Sure. You'll be sleeping there soon enough."

When she hopped up, she almost moaned in relief and pleasure. A pillow top. He'd bought the fluffiest pillow top mattress she'd ever felt, not the hard rectangle of back-wrenching torment she'd expected.

She couldn't resist. She had to do it. And oh, my goddess, it felt amazing.

"What..." He looked at her over his shoulder as he sorted through a drawer. "What the hell are you doing, Lucy?"

"I'm making a duvet angel." She stopped, leaving her arms and legs stretched spread-eagle across the most amazing bed in existence. "I couldn't resist. This is the mattress of the gods, Seb."

The corners of his mouth tucked inward, his secret version of a smile. "I'm glad you approve."

"The princess from The Princess and the Pea? She'd totally be into this bed." She raised herself on one elbow. "She'd move in, and she'd never leave, no matter how many times you tried to convince her to go. It wouldn't matter how many evil stepmothers you recruited to force her out or how many peas you put under the mattress. She'd just dropkick the stepmothers, fish out the peas, and take another nap."

When he laughed, his cheeks creased in the most adorable way. "Dropkicking stepmothers seems a little harsh."

"*Evil* stepmothers. They deserve dropkicking." She sat up and wiggled backward until her shoulders met the headboard. "Besides, I empathize with the princess. I need my rest. Officially, I'm done at my old job, but a few of my favorite clients asked me to keep seeing them until I leave. So I've been planning my move, working, *and* filming this past week."

"Are you meeting your clients at the store?" With quick movements, he gathered a pile of papers from one drawer and shoved them into another, tucking them beneath a stack of sweaters. "Or are you visiting their homes?"

Those papers looked familiar. But how in the world was that possible?

She kept considering the matter as she absently answered his question. "Their homes. The LMT replacing me needs my old space at the store."

"How much do you know about these clients?" He was transporting a dark pile of...something...now. Underwear?

She squinted, but couldn't quite tell. Dammit.

Back to that pile of papers. It had included lined paper, from what she'd seen, mixed with normal printer paper. All filled with writing. A few smaller rectangles, including one with a picture of a—

Wait. She knew what those papers were. No wonder he'd wanted her to hang out in the living room while he dealt with the drawers.

"I've read their intake paperwork, and I've seen most of them for years." She tilted her head, wondering at what those papers revealed about him. "If I didn't trust them, I wouldn't have agreed to go to their homes."

"So you think it's safe."

Ah, the old Sebastián had returned, his expression and tone both determinedly neutral. But the past twenty-four hours had revealed more about him than he probably realized.

"I *know* it's safe."

He nodded. "Fair enough. You have good instincts."

She let that firm statement warm her thoroughly before she spoke again. "Hey, Seb?"

"Yeah?" He looked up from a second nearly-empty drawer.

"Two quick questions."

He straightened and turned toward her. "Shoot."

"How's your head doing?" Not that he'd tell her if he were in pain, but she needed to ask.

"Fine," he said, to her total lack of surprise. "What's your second question?"

She rested against the headboard and watched his face. "Why did you keep all the letters and postcards and e-mails I've sent you over the years?"

FOUR

Later that night, sleepless and unsettled on his lumpy-ass pullout couch, Sebastián considered the damning evidence Lucy had seen.

His request—no, his *plea*—for her to stay with him had revealed more than enough. Too much. But he could dismiss that moment of weakness as the justifiable concern of a casual friend for her comfort and safety. The stash of letters, on the other hand...

Stupid turtle postcard, he thought. *You gave me away, you green-finned motherfucker.*

He'd never intended for Lucy to know how he'd printed all her e-mails in case he switched providers or accidentally erased his old messages or experienced some sort of worldwide computer outage. How he'd moved that stack of letters with him across the country. How he'd kept those postcards, those neatly penned lines, those smiley-face-laden e-mails hidden but close to him. Protected from view and harm both.

For all his attempts to downplay the significance of that stash, to brush it off as the instinct of a data-driven engineer, he'd spied new knowledge in her warm brown eyes. Speculation. Unwelcome questions about him and the intensity of his feelings for her.

For well over a decade, he'd managed to hide himself. She'd never comprehended that she was his greatest joy, as well as his greatest vulnerability.

And he didn't reveal vulnerabilities to anyone.

Not even to Lucy. Not even during those few, breathless moments over the years when he'd have sworn she felt the same way about him. Not even when she smiled at him and he wanted to shout his love for her to the world.

He'd trained himself too well. Or maybe his years at Marysburg High had done the job for him. Either way, he'd learned his lesson.

Expose your heart, and someone would crush it underfoot.

But how much longer could he hide that heart from the one woman who'd always owned it?

BEFORE FIRST LIGHT, HE'D ALREADY MADE COFFEE and given Hairy—ineffably stupid but sweet, as always—a walk, some food, and a good rub. Then he'd almost tripped on the damn dog, who seemed intent on remaining underfoot when he wasn't sniffing after poor Kitty, who lay exhausted, cranky, and well-licked on her least-despised blanket.

Once Sebastián worked up the courage, he crept into his bedroom, cursing his idiocy. If he hadn't gotten so rattled last night, he'd have remembered to grab the necessary clothing and toiletries for the next day.

Lucy needed her sleep. He didn't want to wake her. If he didn't particularly want to face her either, that was an entirely irrelevant issue.

But her eyes were open when he cracked the bedroom door, and she sat up. "Morning, Seb."

In his bed, she looked just as he'd sometimes dreamed. Sleepy, rumpled, and warm. Soft and relaxed and happy to see him. Gorgeous.

The covers fell to her waist as she flicked her hair behind her shoulders. She'd worn an oversized tee to bed. Innocuous enough. And her bralessness, while welcome, wasn't exactly a change from her normal attire. But he knew for a fact she wasn't wearing one of her voluminous skirts, since yesterday's offering lay draped over her suitcase.

Those bare, curvy legs were tangled in his sheets right now, and he couldn't breathe.

Was she wearing any underwear at all? Or would she be warm and naked all over if he tugged aside the covers?

Shit. *Stop staring, man. You're being creepy and weird.*

"Good morning." He cleared his throat, trying to make his tone convey his total lack of interest in the sexy woman lying in his bed while possibly panty-less and definitely braless. "I forgot my clothing. I'll be out of your way in a second."

She propped a pillow in front of the headboard and scooted back against it. "No problem. Take your time."

Then, to his dismay, she just watched him. And damn it, his fingers kept fumbling with the drawer handles and the things he needed, like underwear and socks.

"I haven't seen you shirtless since high school." Her smile contained a hint of naughtiness he hadn't spied in far too long. "You look good in a pair of pajama bottoms, Castillo."

He had to smile. "You haven't really seen me shirtless now either. Without your glasses, I'm just a man-shaped blur."

"I can see better than you think."

He wasn't touching that loaded statement. "Once I grab

my toiletries, I'll leave you in peace. There's still plenty of time to sleep before we have to go."

"I'd like to doze a little longer." Her back arched in a sinuous stretch, and he almost swallowed his tongue. "But Hairy is probably squirming and crossing his legs by now, so I'd better get up."

"I took care of that. You can relax."

He darted into the bathroom, snatched a handful of random bottles, and raced for the door to the hall. Before long, the state of his pajama bottoms would be obvious even to a woman with severe myopia. He needed to flee. Now.

She flopped down onto her back again. "Thank you so much. In that case, I really am going back to sleep. Could you wake me an hour before we have to leave?"

"Sure."

The door was almost closed when she spoke again. "Seb?"

Oh, Jesus. Not another *quick question*. His heart would implode.

He couldn't speak. Instead, he simply waited.

"If you looked in my suitcase…" She paused. "If you looked in there, you'd see a bunch of papers too. Every terrible limerick you ever wrote me. Even the high school one about Allie, where you rhymed *Alyssa* with *ass-kissa* and *diss-a*. I put them all in a binder years ago."

She'd packed her unnecessary items and moved them into storage. Did that mean she considered all those awful literary offerings, written solely for her amusement…necessary?

Did that mean she considered *him* necessary? As necessary as he considered her? But if so, why was she moving?

She didn't say any more, and he didn't ask. Instead, he closed the door quietly behind him and fed his disgruntled cat while trying very hard not to think about how easy joining Lucy in bed would have been.

Two hours later, he was still trying. Even the sight of her

fully dressed—or as fully dressed as she ever got, anyway—didn't stave off the wholesale lust that had overtaken him in the past twenty-four hours.

Outside his dreams, he'd never let himself think about her in such a sexual way before. Never, not when his need for her company was already so powerful. Not when his desire could weaken his resolve to keep his feelings hidden. Now, though…

Now he couldn't seem to stop.

She mentioned how hot and tight the loft yesterday had been, and he placed himself behind a strategic kitchen counter. She checked the bump on his head, and he wanted to capture those careful, gentle fingers in his mouth. She drifted into the sunlight pouring through his window, and his eyes focused on her sweet, small nipples without any say-so from his conscious brain.

Until yesterday, he'd been a man under complete control. This was a travesty.

After a quick breakfast, they gave Hairy one last rub and Kitty one last respectful nod, and then headed out the door. Soon, thank God, they weren't going to be alone anymore. Surrounded by the show's crew, he should be able to regain his equilibrium without any problem.

Neutral. Stay neutral.

That vow of neutrality lasted until they rounded a corner and the next tiny house option came into view, Allie and the crew standing beside it.

His hands clenched on the wheel. "Jesus Christ."

"I think Jesus abandoned that school bus a few years ago." She sounded amused but tired. "I appreciate the sentiment, however."

He parked a good distance from the crew, buying him and Lucy time to talk privately. "You're very calm about the prospect of Allie pressuring you to buy…that."

That rust-ridden monstrosity, he wanted to add. But Lucy needed to draw her own conclusions.

"When I couldn't go back to sleep this morning, I meditated for a while." Her hand had delved into her pocket, and he knew she was rubbing her amethyst again. Her glasses she might misplace, but never her worry stone. "I decided to stay in the moment and enjoy today."

He nodded. "Good."

Until Jarrod, that was how she'd always dealt with her daily life and its stresses: with meditation, warm enthusiasm, and faith that the future would take care of itself if she paid attention to the present. As she'd once explained to him, the worry stone served as a way to ground herself in her senses and bring herself back to the now. It wasn't meant to be a crutch, but a reminder.

He wasn't sure it still fulfilled the same purpose these days. After Jarrod, she'd begun to doubt herself, question her own decisions, in a way Sebastián had never seen before. And each time she reached for that worry stone now, the pit of rage in his stomach burned a little hotter.

Not rage at her. Never her.

At that dick she'd dated. At a world that had dimmed her glow, when she was better than all of them. Jarrod. Allie. Sebastián himself.

He would give anything to have that inimitable Lucy shine back. Now.

"Unlike yesterday, I already know what to expect." She unhooked her seat belt. "If this…um, peach-colored bus doesn't suit my needs, I know I'll find something that does. I can make this situation work, one way or the other."

Cracking his car door, he swung a foot onto the parking lot pavement.

"And unlike yesterday, I won't forget the most important part." She got out and closed the door behind her. "I'm spending time with you, my favorite person in the world. That's cause for joy and gratitude, no matter what the day brings."

Her smile rivaled the sun. He drew in a deep breath, tempted to drop to his knees and give thanks for everything she was. To beg her not to leave him, even though he'd never even hinted that he wanted her to stay.

Instead, he walked beside her to the bus and the waiting crew. And after the hair and makeup lady got through with them both and the cameras and boom mic had been positioned to Jill's satisfaction, they were back to filming.

"This converted school bus comes in two thousand dollars below your budget, and it boasts 245 square feet of charming living space." Allie swept a hand toward the bus. "No tiny house could be more portable!"

Lucy shaded her eyes with her hand as she considered the vehicle. "Would I need a commercial driver's license to bring this with me from state to state?"

"I researched that." Allie appeared pleased to have been asked the question. "Once a bus has been converted for personal use, you don't need a special license, although some states may ask you to get a special endorsement."

"Okay." Lucy didn't mention the weird paint color or the rusty spots. Instead, she nodded calmly toward the bus entrance. "Shall we go inside?"

To be fair, the inside of the bus seemed much less cramped than yesterday's cabin. The passenger seats had all been removed, leaving space for a small living area, a bare-bones kitchen, a private bathroom, and a sunny bedroom in the back of the bus.

All good things. However...

"Is this"—Lucy stepped closer to one of the walls and touched a gray lump with her fingertip—"old gum?"

"What a creative way to add texture to a wall treatment,

right?" Allie hustled past that spot—and dozens of similar spots on the floors and walls—and toward the bathroom. "I think you'll like this area of the house."

But Lucy hadn't budged. Instead, she was staring at a mark on the wall near the gum, her brows drawn together. He moved beside her and got a better view of the mark's shape.

Oh. *Oh.*

Well, given the previous use of the bus, perhaps they should have expected as much.

Lucy scanned the wall and ceiling, squatting to study other marks closer to the floor. Then her peaceful expression fractured, and she started giggling.

"Allie…" Her body was shaking with her laughter, her brown eyes bright. "D-did you see what's all over the walls?"

Allie bit her lip. "This bus features many fine examples of outsider art. It's truly an outstanding value."

"Outsider art? Is that what people are calling these now?" Lucy snorted. "When we went to school, I believe they were just dick drawings. Lots and lots of dick drawings."

"Cut!" Jill yelled.

After a moment, Lucy managed to calm herself. "I apologize, Jill. I just hadn't anticipated so many penises"—she snorted again—"in my potential house."

He couldn't help himself. "Don't neglect the balls."

She bent over laughing again. "Y-you're right. I was wrong to ignore the lovely, h-hairy balls also included in the drawings."

Like him, Jill and the crew were snickering to themselves. Even Allie, to his surprise, had cracked a smile.

"The cameras won't focus on the, uh, outsider art." After wiping her eyes, Jill got back to business. "As long as you don't use the term *dick drawings*, though, feel free to talk about what you see."

"What term should I use instead?" Lucy raised her brows. "Penis pictorals? Tumescent tracings? Sack-related sketches?"

The sparkle was returning. He could almost see her brighten, minute by minute.

Jill waved a hand. "Whatever you want. Alliterate away. Just no dicks, pricks, or cocks, please."

He could have sworn he heard Lucy mutter, "Speak for yourself."

But then the cameras were rolling again, and they were moving toward the miniature kitchen. As they went, he scanned overhead and beneath his feet. No additional insulation, as far as he could see. Patched original floors. Gum and dicks everywhere. Whoever had converted the bus hadn't devoted a great deal of money or care to the process.

The kitchen area appeared workable, however. A square of tiled counter, a small sink, and four electric burners on the stovetop. The tiny oven might even be able to fit a tofu turkey, if Lucy shoved it in there hard enough.

"This kitchen features everything you need for Thanksgiving dinner," Allie declared.

Lucy opened the oven door and glanced inside. He stooped beside her, and she turned her head to whisper to him. "No dicks in the oven. I'm kind of disappointed, to be honest."

"Cut," Jill called again. "Lucy, the mic is more sensitive than you'd imagine."

Lucy bit her lip, but couldn't stop herself from responding. "As are dicks."

For that, he high-fived her. "Nice."

"Don't encourage me." She stood again. "I'm sorry, everyone. I'll get a hold of myself, I promise."

Manfully resisting a *get a hold* joke, he composed his expression once more.

"Why don't you two do what I call the butt-bump test?"

The producer pointed to the stove. "Lucy, you stand in front of there like you're cooking. Sebastián, you stand at the café table across from the oven. Face the windows and pretend you're eating breakfast or something. Let's see if you have enough room to work without bumping butts."

He and Lucy got into position. The crew began filming again. And sure enough, when Lucy opened the oven and pretended to put something inside, they were touching, just as Jill had predicted.

Lucy's soft, rounded bottom pressed up against him, and the world dropped away.

"I think this stove would work for me," she said, a bit breathless.

Oh, fuck, he loved her ass. Always had. Even back in high school, when he'd only appreciated it in a platonic way, he'd acknowledged its superiority over all other asskind. Her sweet breasts might be small, but her booty and hips...they were lush. Profligate and welcoming.

His appreciation could no longer be termed platonic. Not in any universe.

He tried to back away from the amazing, horrible contact, but there was nowhere to go, not without messing up the shot. And the camera operators kept saying they needed a different angle or that the mic had malfunctioned, so there they were, butt-to-butt, for minutes on end, as Lucy moved a bit from side to side, pretending to work in the kitchen as she chatted with Allie.

It felt like a tease. It felt like heaven and a very specific kind of hell.

Seemingly years later, Jill spoke again. "Good. Let's set up the next shot in the bathroom. FYI, Lucy, the shower is kind of small. I have no idea how a larger person would fit in there. Or two people, for that matter."

"Maybe we should..." Lucy blinked up at him. "Maybe we

should test that out? In case I ever had, um, special company?"

She wanted to know whether she could fuck in the shower? He could show her. He'd be *delighted* to show her. Even if the space was too tight for full-on penetration, he could get to his knees and brace her against the wall, her legs over his shoulders as he—

No. No, no, no. He dropped his chin to his chest and took a breath. *Friends. You're friends. Don't let her know you want anything more.*

So he crowded into the tiny, surprisingly clean shower stall with her, cameras rolling, and prayed that she—and they—couldn't detect his reaction to such potent temptation. MATLAB simulations. He'd think of MATLAB simulations, rather than the press of her breasts against his chest or the sounds she'd make when he licked her open under the shower spray and sucked her clit so gently into his mouth—

"Seb?" she whispered. "You smell really good. Do you use cologne or aftershave or…?"

"Umm…" He couldn't remember. At this point, he probably smelled like nothing but pheromones and desperation. "Not sure what I used this morning."

"Maybe if we"—she rubbed against him as she slipped her arms around his waist, and his eyes nearly rolled back in his head—"maneuver a little, we'll be a bit more comfortable. Just give me a moment."

Hell. He really had descended to the fiery depths of Hades, where well-intentioned men who were trying their best to control their emotions and their disobedient cocks got tortured for their efforts.

For a decade and a half, he'd kept things light. Casual. Made sure he didn't reveal the intensity of his feelings or how they'd shifted with the years and puberty.

And this was how he got rewarded? Motherfucker.

She was still squirming, her softness breathtaking against him as those agile massage therapist's hands slid from his back to his shoulders. "Nearly there. I just need to—"

When her elbow hit the shower handle and icy water poured down on them both, he was almost grateful.

FIVE

As they lay together on the bed, Lucy made sure she spoke directly into Sebastián's ear, cognizant by now of just how sensitive that damned boom mic was. "We're basically in the dick-lover's Sistine Chapel. You realize that, right?"

Okay, maybe she wasn't getting so close only because of the mic.

She wanted her mouth near him. She wanted her mouth on him. And holy goddess of fiery lust, she wanted his mouth on *her*, anywhere and everywhere.

He hadn't relaxed since that first butt-to-butt contact earlier in the day. His shoulders had bunched into round masses, and that vein in his temple kept throbbing, throbbing, throbbing. He was either really irritated, really uncomfortable, or really turned on.

The problem: She didn't know which. And he wouldn't tell her.

She'd gotten a sense of his physical state in the shower, but that could have been fleeting and impersonal, the generic reaction of a straight man pressed up against a woman. An erection, as she knew, didn't mean much. It was a physical response to stimuli, not a sign of specific desire or deeper emotions. Without the context Sebastián wouldn't give her, it meant nothing more than those scrawled drawings of dicks.

And balls, she quickly added. *Mustn't neglect the balls.*

"I'm trying to appreciate this singular cultural opportunity." His voice was bone-dry, and his body against hers was tense and exuding heat, despite the lingering dampness of their clothing. "I hadn't expected the kids to create such a masterpiece on the ceiling of the back of the bus. Consider me impressed by the level of detail and the sheer quantity of penises."

"Michelangelo could have taken some lessons." She grinned. "He missed an amazing opportunity to replace those touching fingers with something else, for example."

When a rare chuckle rumbled in his chest, she shifted to see his expression and almost fell off the bed. His left arm flashed out just in time, though, catching her and pulling her back against him.

"Thank you." She stayed on her side, facing him. If one of her breasts was now nudging his arm, well, that wasn't her fault. It was an issue of safety, above all. "I don't want to land on that floor."

He tried to move closer to the wall, but there was nowhere to go. "Understandably."

The bed—which, having learned their lesson from the Hashish Hideaway, they'd covered with Sebastián's tarp before testing—really wasn't big enough for two people. Nevertheless, she'd again mentioned the possibility of *special company* and requested they try to fit in it together.

She was growing quite fond of her *special company* tests. The cameras and mic and people surrounding them, less so. And the bed felt like a slab of concrete beneath her.

In her opinion, though, it was still a vast improvement

over the Loft of Head Trauma. "So what do you think about this bedroom, compared to the loft?"

His response was measured and neutral, as always. "What I think doesn't matter."

But it did. In more ways than she could express.

"Please." She lifted up on an elbow to catch his eye. "I want your opinion. I promise I won't let it override mine."

When she asked him for something, he didn't often refuse her. This time was no exception.

"This mattress probably originated as a torture device in the Spanish Inquisition." He repositioned himself and winced. "But for a variety of reasons, I prefer this bedroom."

"Because we didn't have to climb a rock wall to get here, and I'm less likely to brain myself with every attempt to sit upright?"

"That's part of it."

The lump under his cool, thick hair felt smaller, thank goddess. After she checked the evidence of injury, she let her fingers linger and play with the silky strands. "I'm so sorry you got hurt helping me."

He shifted his shoulders. "It's fine. At least I have a few more days off to recover before I return to work next week."

"True." She lowered her hand and rested it on his chest. "So why else do you prefer this bedroom?"

At the question, his heart rate noticeably increased beneath her palm. She frowned, concerned.

"It doesn't matter," he said.

She was increasingly unwilling to accept that pat, easy answer. "It does. Tell me." Spreading her fingers, she tried to infuse all her affection, all her sincerity into her touch. Maybe that physical connection could reach his heart, even if her words didn't. "Please."

"I can't."

He raised his head and looked at both cameras recording

their every move, the boom mic registering their every word. At some point in the last few seconds, she'd forgotten about them, forgotten about everyone and everything else but Sebastián.

Yet another unnecessary interruption would probably infuriate Allie. It might even nudge Jill from indulgence to impatience. But the man beside her was worth a little trouble.

She caught Jill's eye. "Can we stop filming for a minute?"

The camera operators looked to the producer, who nodded. "Let's take five and give them some privacy. I think we got plenty of usable footage."

"Can't you talk after filming is done? This was supposed to be the next-to-last shot of the day." Allie stood near the bed, hands on her hips. "Let's wrap things up."

Jill's voice was firm. "I agreed to Lucy's request. Please give them a few minutes alone, Allie."

Her mouth pinched tight, Allie strode away, the crew close behind her. The bus grew quiet. And when Lucy turned back to Sebastián, that shallow furrow had appeared between his brows.

Maybe she shouldn't keep touching him. Shouldn't propose these *special company* tests. Shouldn't push him to share more of himself, body and soul, when she might upend the foundation of their friendship by doing so.

But time was running out. She was leaving in a matter of weeks, and she didn't expect to return to Marysburg anytime soon. If she didn't take her chances now, she'd likely never know what he really felt, much less what they could be together. She'd never know whether she should have postponed her trip to Minneapolis, or even canceled it entirely.

He was worth the risk. *They* were worth the risk.

So she smoothed away that furrow between his brows with a fingertip. "Tell me."

"In school, I..." His throat bobbed as he swallowed. "I got shoved into a lot of lockers. A lot of closets too. Which is a cliché, but it happened."

Oh, no. She knew now where this was leading, and her heart folded in two.

She levered herself over him, positioning her body so she was resting full-length on top of him, a human blanket. "You couldn't get out."

"They were dark. And really tight, even for a small kid like me." He took a shuddering breath beneath her. "I sometimes...um, panicked."

"Of course you did. Anyone would." She cupped his cheek. "I'm so sorry."

When they'd attended Marysburg High together, the school had been overcrowded, underfunded, and understaffed. Unless parents chose to raise an enormous fuss, things like bullying had gone largely unnoticed and unpunished. She'd alerted trustworthy teachers to the incidents she'd seen, but Sebastián had refused to share his story. And she knew her friend. He would have convinced his parents to let the matter go, if they'd even known about the bullies in the first place.

"Don't apologize. You tried to help." His breathing became deeper again, slower. "I wouldn't let you."

"Does this space bother you?" Despite the relatively high ceilings, the bus owner had squeezed the bedroom into a small area, and she didn't yet understand the extent of Sebastián's claustrophobia. "I'll get up, so you can have some breathing room."

When she tried to move, his arms wrapped around her, holding her in place. "No. I'm fine here. And having you with me changes things."

"How?" She let herself drape over him once more. Her ear rested on his chest, and his heartbeat, strong and steady, echoed in her head. "I chatter so much that you can't think?"

Jarrod had told her that. He hadn't meant it as a compliment.

Sebastián's hand slid slowly up her spine. He gave the nape of her neck a gentle squeeze, while his other hand rested at the small of her back, heavy and warm.

The touch was pure comfort and pure excitement at the same time.

"Whether you talk or not, you're a potent distraction, Lucy." His fingers probed at her neck muscles, finding tension and kneading it away. "And hearing your voice is usually the highlight of my day."

She stilled beneath his hands. For years, she'd assumed her occasional wistful imaginings were one-sided. But now…

Raising her head, she looked down at him. His lips were parted, his eyes dark and heavy-lidded. Heat streaked across his cheekbones, and beneath her that predictable physical reaction had occurred again. Because he wanted her? Or because a woman, any woman, was lying atop him?

He offered her a small smile. "There once was a girl from Virginny, who looked at a bus that was mini. She saw many big dicks, and for one final trick, against her friend's fears she did win-ny."

"Holy fuck, Seb." She buried her face against his shirt and laughed. "That may be your worst limerick yet. You rhymed *Virginny* and *win-ny*."

When she raised her head again, he was laughing too. "Also, the bus isn't actually mini, but such are the compromises of literary genius."

His face had lit with amusement, his cheeks creased in that adorable way she'd seen far too few times, and never in such close proximity. His expression was open and unguarded, and he'd just shared more of himself with her than ever before.

In that moment, Sebastián Castillo was the most beautiful sight she'd ever witnessed. Nothing else could compare. Not sparkling Hawaiian waterfalls or snowcapped Alps or lush Caribbean rain forests. Not smooth orbs of amethyst or hearts carved of rose quartz.

Still smiling, she leaned forward. And before she could change her mind, she pressed her mouth to his for the first time in over fifteen years of friendship.

He froze in place. She took a split second to appreciate the plush give of his lips beneath hers, the startled rush of his breath, and the exciting brush of stubble against her cheeks. The warm scent of sage and sea salt she'd noticed that day. The way he tasted like mint and—something. Like Sebastián, she supposed. Like the safest place she'd ever been.

Then she moved to his side before the kiss turned from plausibly platonic to undeniably erotic. She'd signaled her willingness. If he wanted more, he'd have to take it. He'd have to say something, do something. He'd have to take a chance and trust them both.

Chest tight, she waited for him to reach out and grab hold of her.

But he didn't. Instead, he clambered out of the bed and strode outside, his face flushed but unreadable once more.

She gathered the tarp, palmed her worry stone, and followed him, pasting on a smile for their audience.

Of course he hadn't grabbed hold of her. Her conviction that he wanted her as more than a friend couldn't be trusted, because her judgment couldn't be trusted. She was silly and naïve and confused, as she'd been told many times before.

She should have known he wouldn't reach for her. But it still hurt that he hadn't.

And since she had no desire to experience that pain or overstep the bounds of friendship again, she wasn't reaching for him a second time, whatever her foolish heart might insist. Period.

As soon as Hairy caught sight of Sebastián's house, he began barking and leaping toward the door, like the deluded, lovesick dog he was.

She held the leash tight. Much as she hated to stymie him, she needed a few more moments before venturing inside that featureless, gray front door. Before facing an evening all alone with Sebastián and their mismatched pets.

Nothing has changed. The two of you are still friends. You're still moving across the country. You still need to find a place to live before you go. Focus on the important bits, not on distractions.

An hour-long session with a client, a bit of meditation, and this long walk with Hairy had done her a world of good, as always. And although living in the same house as Sebastián for the next week or so might not be the optimal way to move past her disappointment, he didn't deserve blame for her overactive imagination.

In fact, he deserved thanks for taking her and her now pitifully whimpering dog into his home for an indeterminate number of days. She knew how she could show her appreciation.

It was going to hurt, though. For both of them.

She closed her eyes and thought about all he'd done for her, all he'd been to her, and waited until her fake smile became genuine. Then she let herself into the unlocked door, took off Hairy's leash, and faced her friend.

Sebastián was sitting on the couch, his unreadable eyes on her. "You were gone a long time."

"You live in a great neighborhood for walking." She toed off her shoes, loath to damage his gleaming wooden floors. "We ended up going farther than I'd expected, just because it's such a nice evening out."

He acknowledged her words with a little nod. "I wondered whether you'd gotten lost."

Hairy had bounded directly toward Kitty's sleeping spot. But he must have learned some discretion overnight, since he only gave her two long licks before backing just out of paw's reach. To Lucy's shock, the cat didn't hiss or yowl in response. Instead, she stretched on her little bed, got to her feet, and padded over to the golden retriever. Just before she'd have bumped into him, she twisted, flicked him with her tail, and presented him with her ass as she stalked away.

"For Kitty, that's a declaration of love." When Hairy tried to follow her and she gave him a halfhearted swipe to the nose, Sebastián amended, "A reluctant, conflicted love that might require stitches at some point, but love nonetheless."

"So they're set for the next hour or so, right?"

His brows pinched a millimeter. "I put out food and water for both of them, yes. Why?"

"Sit at the table, please. Unless you'd rather do this lying down." She considered the matter. "And I need to know if you want me to use oil."

His lips parted, and his brows shot skyward. "Uhh... Are you sure you..." He paused, cheeks flushed, and then tried again. "What?"

"You're tight. I felt it earlier today." Why was he giving her that dazed look? "The pain from your head injury is making you tense your shoulders, or possibly the stress of being on camera. Or maybe that pull-out couch from last night."

Pursing his lips, he bowed his head. "My shoulders. Right."

"So I'll give you a massage. But you need to decide whether you want me to tackle just your back and shoulders or your full b—"

"Back and shoulders." His voice was urgent. "Just back and shoulders."

"Because we could use your bed, if you want a full-body massage without oil. If you do want me to use oil, I'll grab my massage table from my car." She'd left it in there after her session that afternoon. "Otherwise, things can get slippery and stain your sheets."

Yeesh, he looked pained. His shoulders must really be hurting. Maybe his head too?

He held up his hands. "On second thought, I'm fine. I don't need a massage or oil or a bed. Thank y—"

"I insist." She refused to back down, not when her generous friend could use her talents. Especially since he'd never, ever ask for help, even when he needed it. "I'm so grateful you gave us a place to stay."

He wet his lips with a quick swipe of his tongue, and she couldn't look away. "But you must be tired. We filmed for most of the morning and early afternoon, and then you had a session. If anything, *you* should get a massage."

"I'm fine. And I know a few ways to help myself relax." She wiggled her fingers. "I have talented hands."

His cheeks had darkened with his flush. Was he really so embarrassed to accept assistance?

"I'm sure you do," he said.

"I can massage a few key spots myself."

His chin dropped to his chest. "Okay."

"I also have a foam roller I can use."

"How does a foam r—" He shook his head. "Never mind. My point is that I don't need a massage, but I very much appreciate the offer. Now let's discuss dinner options."

"Please, Seb." She put all her conviction into the words. "I want to do this for you. To feel like I'm contributing in some way."

"I don't know." For once, his emotions had carved themselves so deeply onto his face, even a stranger could have read them. Reluctance. Worry. Longing. "This may not be a good idea."

"It'll be fine. I got a good night's sleep last night, thanks to you, so I have plenty of energy. And if you let me get my hands on you, I swear you'll feel better." She wiggled her fingers again. "I know what I'm doing."

His eyes shut tight for a moment. "I believe you."

"So?"

The answer was a long time coming. "Okay."

"Okay?" She grinned at him, delighted. "As in, okay, I can give you a massage?"

With a sigh, he opened his eyes and nodded. "Let's do this."

SIX

Sebastián didn't understand quite how it had happened. Somehow, he appeared to be sitting at his own kitchen table, naked from the waist up, oiled like a particularly shiny extra in the movie *300*, considerable pain radiating through various parts of his body, with Lucy's hands all over him.

She used her elbow to combat a tough knot in his left shoulder, and he almost wept. To his dismay, he did let out a sort of grunt.

Maybe more of a whimper, if he were being honest about it.

She paused in her torture. "You okay?"

"Fine," he managed to grit out.

It was a daydream that had twisted into a nightmare. He was half-naked, and Lucy was touching him, but he couldn't touch her back, and she apparently harbored a heretofore unknown tendency toward sadism.

Worst of all? Despite the agony, he still had an erection. His cock had perked up at the first touch of Lucy's fingertips on his bare skin. Not even her knuckles, or—God help him—

her sharp, sharp elbows, could dissuade it from its considerable enthusiasm.

His cock was basically Hairy Garcia, only less likely to be petted by Lucy.

At that thought, it strained at the leash of his pants again.

"With most clients, I'd work up to this level of pressure, but we don't have months of sessions ahead of us. I need to give you as much relief as possible, as quickly as possible. Plus, you said you wanted it hard."

Oh, he did. He really did.

That kiss on the bed had almost broken him. Before she'd moved to his side, he'd been one millisecond away from dragging her beneath him and sliding a hand under that convenient skirt of hers. And fuck, when she'd imposed distance between them, he'd wanted to snatch her back against him and erase those hateful inches.

But he wouldn't make more of a friendly kiss than was warranted. She might not have ever demonstrated her affection in quite that way before, but it wasn't out of character for her. Not surprisingly for a massage therapist, she was a toucher. Always had been. She nudged, she hugged, she high-fived, she poked, and apparently she kissed too.

It wasn't her fault that his body and emotions misinterpreted innocent gestures.

He could have sworn something dark and pained had dawned in her soft eyes when he'd walked away, though. Something like what he felt every time he thought about her leaving.

It doesn't matter. No matter how she feels, you've shown and told her too much already.

Maybe a little conversation would calm his confused body. Worth a shot, he guessed. "How did your session go this afternoon?"

Her hands paused, and he tried not to cheer. Although he

had to admit it: When he rolled his shoulders now, they felt…different. Loose. Weightless. Like she'd lightened the burden there, just like she'd lightened all the other burdens in his life.

Except his stupid intransigent erection, of course.

"—normal, except at the end."

He sat up straight. "Did your client say something inappropriate? Or touch you?"

Because he might not have fought anyone since high school graduation, but he kept in shape and had taken boxing lessons. He'd gladly wade into the fray for Lucy again, no more questions asked.

She gave him a little smack on his shoulder, and God, his dick was really confused right now.

"Of course not," she said, her exasperation clear. "I told you these clients were trustworthy. No, he just wanted to buy a gift certificate as a present."

"What's abnormal about that?"

"Well…" Her elbow pressed into that knot again, and he almost howled. "He works at Colonial Marysburg, right? One of those people in colonial costume. But I swear to goddess, Seb, the dude has money. Lots of money. He lives in a mansion, as I found out today. And the woman who calls to make his appointments once referred to herself as his butler. Not his assistant, his *butler*. And she backtracked quickly, but really. What kind of costumed interpreter can afford a mansion? Or an assistant, much less one with pretensions of butler-related grandeur?"

"So maybe he doesn't have to work, but wants to." Propping his own elbows on the table, he covered his face with his hands. "I still don't see the abnormal bit."

"I'm getting there. Anyway, so Adam wanted this gift certificate, but I reminded him I'm leaving soon. He said that was okay, because he planned to tell the recipient she'd won a contest and would have to redeem the prize—my certificate—within the next week. And I was supposed to go along with his story, no matter how *incredibly, awe-inspiringly cranky* she got. His words, by the way."

Sebastián frowned. "That is weird. Why not just give the certificate directly to her?"

"Exactly what I asked. But he told me that was how it had to be, and I wasn't willing to push him. I haven't been seeing him for long, but he's a good tipper, Seb. I mean, a *really* good tipper."

"Did you agree to his request?"

"Of course. If he wants to give an anonymous gift, in however weird a way, I don't see the harm. He even covered her tip." She started massaging his temples with those strong fingers, and he tried not to moan in pleasure. "So I'm expecting a phone call from a cantankerous colonial woman who thinks she won a contest, but hasn't, and who needs to schedule a massage within the next week, all due to the machinations of a butler-having colonial dude who tips a hundred percent, lives in a mansion, and smells like an expensive tropical vacation."

His brows drew together. She'd noticed how this guy *smelled?*

"So it was a bit weird, as I was saying." She was working on his neck now, digging her thumbs into either side of his spine. "But entertaining."

"Are you seeing him again before you leave?" If so, he planned to accompany her and wait in the car during the appointment. The guy sounded like a weirdo. A good-smelling weirdo with philanthropic tendencies, but a weirdo nevertheless.

"Nope. No time. " She patted Sebastián on the shoulder. "How are you feeling?"

"Good." To his surprise, it was even the truth. "Really good. Looser."

She grinned. "All in a day's work. Just make sure to drink lots of water tonight."

He pulled on his tee without delay, oily sheen be damned. Fully dressed once more, he rose to get each of them a glass of ice water, but paused when she settled herself into the chair next to his.

Time to see whether Lucy had been fibbing earlier.

As she let the seat take her weight, she made an almost inaudible noise and stretched her back just a bit. If he hadn't been watching her so closely—if he didn't *always* watch her so closely—he'd never have noticed either telltale signal.

But he had, and he did. She was hurting.

For all her talk about a good night's sleep, she'd been on her feet the entire day. She'd also been lying on a rock-hard school bus mattress. And he knew her last conversation with Allie had bothered her more than she chose to admit. Her quasi-friend had not taken the rejection of the bus well, despite Lucy's sound reasoning. It needed too many repairs and modifications for Lucy's budget, ease of transport notwithstanding.

Plus, there were all the dicks. So, so many dicks.

So she'd spurned the school bus, politely but with more firmness and conviction than he'd seen from her in a while, and she'd remained unswayed by Allie's displeasure.

Something about the tiny-house selection process, ridiculous as it was, seemed to have helped her. Maybe how it forced her to focus on her needs and articulate them? To defend them, or else find herself the proud owner of either a nudist stoner's elf cabin or a dick-adorned bus? He didn't know for sure, but something was working for her.

Still, she hated conflict, and she hated disappointing

anyone. Especially a so-called friend, one she'd had since before they could walk.

In other words, he wasn't the only tense, tired person in the house. And she didn't know it—because he'd never told her, for good reason—but she wasn't the only person with massage training in the house either. Hers was much more extensive, of course, but he'd taken a couple of classes. Because, embarrassingly enough, he'd wanted to understand what she did on a daily basis and be able to picture her working at her job.

A smart man would drink his damn water, beat a hasty retreat to the Pullout Couch of the Damned, and pretend to fall asleep shortly after sunset.

But something about the last few days had changed him, too. Whetted his desire for her proximity and her touch. Coaxed him to reveal himself in ways that didn't come easily. Made him question whether all the stringent rules governing his life still made sense.

Goddammit all, she was leaving so fucking soon. Couldn't he allow himself one last taste of the forbidden? Didn't she deserve a friend who would help relieve her pain?

"Why don't I return the favor?" He met her startled gaze, attempting to appear impassive. "I'm no expert, but I should be able to work out a few kinks."

Her brows rose. "Really?"

"Yeah. I, uh"—he swallowed—"took a course or two a few years back."

A hedonist at heart, she didn't hesitate. "That sounds *amazing*. Thank you so much! Where do you want me?"

On the floor. In the chair. On his desk. In the shower. On the bed, for hours at a time.

But he supposed she meant for the massage. "If you'd like me to focus on your shoulders and upper back, the chair. If you'd like me to work on your lower back or legs too, we'll need"—oh, Jesus—"a bed."

"Hmmm." She tapped her lip with her forefinger. "Let's not bother with oil. I just want a gentle massage, and I don't want to have to take another shower tonight. And—"

Thank God for small favors. At least they weren't adding lubrication to this disaster-in-the-making.

"—my feet are aching a bit, so I guess...the bed?" She wrinkled her nose. "Is that okay? Or do you want me to bring in my massage table?"

"The bed is fine."

Why not? It wasn't as if his balls could get any bluer. They'd already reached Horny Smurf status an hour ago.

"Okay." She practically skipped to the bedroom. "Let me get undressed, and I'll be ready in about a minute."

He didn't require a minute. He was already there, Smurftastic balls and all. "Fine."

For the next sixty seconds, he braced himself for whatever state of nakedness Lucy might choose for her massage. She clearly wouldn't be wearing a bra, since he was pretty sure she didn't own one. But what about that loose shirt? Or her skirt? Or—he squeezed his eyes shut—her underwear?

"Ready!" she called out.

Caught between running away and sprinting to her side, he forced himself to walk at a normal, deliberate pace. Only to find her lying on her stomach, topless, her back completely exposed. She'd pushed the skirt up to her thighs, so his eyes could devour almost the full length of her long, strong legs. Maybe she was wearing something else beneath that skirt, maybe she wasn't.

She tucked her hands beneath her cheek. "Is this okay? Because I don't usually wear a skirt during a massage. Do you want me to take it off?"

"*No.*" His hands were shaking. "No, it's fine where it is."

"Okay." She took a deep breath, and the alluring line of her back rose and fell. "Please don't do this for long. I don't want you hurting only minutes after I got you relaxed."

Then he was standing beside the bed, poised to touch her bare skin. Not her hand, or some other innocuous body part countless people had handled in the past, but a private patch of flesh. Paler than her arms, more vulnerable. More intimate.

With the first stroke of his hands over her back, she sighed, and he just about did the same. The warmth of her skin stunned him, its softness echoing her gentle nature. But beneath that smooth skin lay honed, well-used muscles, indicating a strength most people didn't see.

He did. He'd always seen it, from the first moment she'd tugged him away from an incipient fight and forced him to eat lunch with her on a shady patch of grass beside the school. From the first time she'd met his parents and charmed them immediately with her enthusiasm for their unfamiliar dinner offerings. From the first note she'd passed him in class, telling him how much his friendship meant to her.

Again and again, she opened her heart and bared her soul, no matter how the world battered both.

That required strength he couldn't match.

Under his hands, she seemed to melt into the mattress. Her eyes had closed, her golden-brown lashes fanning below them.

"Feels so good," she murmured.

It did. It felt good to give her pleasure. It felt good to touch her in a way that required trust.

"I'm glad." He moved to her legs, using his forearms in long strokes over her strained muscles, and she smiled, her eyes still shut.

"I wrote down the limerick." Her jaw cracked with her yawn. "Your latest masterpiece. Put it in my suitcase."

The stab in his chest forced him to still for a moment. "I'm delighted someone appreciates my wordsmithery."

"Not my favorite, though. The graduation one…" She yawned again. "So sweet."

He'd required weeks to write that limerick, draft after draft discarded for revealing too much or giving her too little of himself. Only the prospect of living halfway across the country from her had allowed him to slip it into her locker the last day of school.

Her cheeks plumped in a tired smile. "My favorite part was how you rhymed *County* with *count-y*. A stroke of genius."

"Creating timeless poetry is hard. Sue me." He rubbed her feet, and her toes wiggled, charming him completely.

"I memorized it." Her voice was getting softer, her words less distinct. "Read it so many times."

He still remembered every line, the tortured product of his struggle to say just enough to show he cared but not enough to show how much.

When she spoke, he could barely hear her. "There once was a girl from Queen's County."

Might as well help her finish. She probably wouldn't even recall the conversation.

"Of kindness she had quite a bounty," he said.

"Then she left for a college…" Her breathing deepened.

"To gain plenty of knowledge." When she didn't reply right away, he filled in the last line for her. "And was missed more than she could count-y."

It was the lone time he'd ever acknowledged missing her, the gaping hole in his life without her in it. When she'd found him later that day, as he was walking home, he could tell she understood the significance.

"I got your note," she'd said, offering a wobbling smile. "How do you count the amount someone is missed? Is there a scale of some sort?"

He'd kicked at the gravel beneath his feet, scared and embarrassed. "I don't know."

"If there is, I'll max it out when we leave in August."

Her eyes bright with tears, she'd tackled him with a hug, squeezing him tight. He'd put his arms around her in return, but hadn't allowed himself to hold on to her with any strength. When she'd pulled away, he hadn't protested or stopped her.

They'd spent another two months together, and then they'd gone their separate ways.

Soon, they'd do it again. And once more, he wasn't holding on tightly.

But maybe he could risk a little more of himself this time. "You were my favorite person in the world. Always were. Always will be."

Sound asleep, she didn't respond. So he covered her, turned out the lights in his bedroom, closed the door behind him, and sat on the couch in the dark, staring into an impossibly empty future.

SEVEN

"Lucy, I remember how much you loved our AP U.S. History class." Allie gestured toward the third tiny house offering. "What a wonderful way to incorporate that enthusiasm into your daily life!"

Lucy had loved biology too, but she didn't plan to live inside a dissected frog anytime soon. Or a deflated kickball, to mark her enjoyment of PE. Still, she had to appreciate the builder's considerable expertise and attention to detail.

"I don't think I've ever seen a more convincing replica of a covered wagon," she said.

Covered wagon replicas, she'd found, were few and far between. Nonexistent, actually, before this very special moment in her life.

"This wagon comes in only four thousand above your top budget, and it's a bargain for the price. Let's go inside and see all the amazing features this tiny house offers." Allie bounded up the wooden steps, the crew following close behind.

Sebastián propped his fists on his hips. "Ah, yes. A

covered wagon tiny house. For when you want to recreate the circumstances of the Donner Party in style."

She didn't think she'd ever heard him offer his opinion quite so freely before. "You don't know. The inside of the wagon could make dying of typhoid or drowning while fording a river look glamorous."

"Yes, maybe this is the Ritz-Carlton of covered wagons. At that price, I'd hope so." His hand rested on the small of her back, warm and strong. "I suppose we should find out for sure."

He'd become considerably more touchy-feely over the past several days. Not even counting that unexpected massage, whose ending she considered decidedly unhappy. After all these years, she'd had his hands on her bare skin and *fallen asleep*?

Shaking her head, she let him nudge her toward the wooden steps. Only to pause inside the front entrance as she registered the wagon's décor. Wood. Wood everywhere, along with dead animals' heads. She'd seen hunting trophies before, but never ones where the poor deer and bears appeared quite so traumatized.

And was that...oh, goddess help them both.

Sebastián leaned over her shoulder to read the inscription below the ax and knife collection mounted to the wall. "'For when the tiny house hunter becomes the tiny house hunted.' Huh."

"The trophies are removable, of course." Allie didn't make eye contact with any of the animals. "That should provide ample wall space for additional storage. Although the seller offered to include them in the sale for an additional fee."

"Whatever you do, don't look into the stew pot," he whispered into Lucy's ear, the tickle of his breath delicious. "It may contain the remains of previous potential buyers. Or maybe the other members of the wagon train."

"The dry sink is so convenient for washing." Allie had moved a few steps further into the wagon. "This is a fantastic opportunity to live off the grid."

Licking her lips, Lucy attempted to interpret real estate agent code. "Does that mean there's no running water or electricity in this wagon?"

"Not..." Allie's shoulders slumped. "Not at the moment. But just look at the beautiful wood carvings the owner incorporated into the master trundle bed. How clever to put a bed beneath a bench!"

Sebastián's eyebrows rose. "The *master* trundle bed? Is there a second one for guests?"

Allie straightened and glared at him. "No. But—"

"Unless I'm mistaken," he interrupted, his voice low and tight, "those carvings appear to depict a man slaughtering his enemies in their sleep."

"That's..." Her swallow was audible. "That's correct."

Given how much Lucy hated arguments, she should really intervene before the antagonism between Allie and Sebastián mounted further. Then again, it turned out she also hated Covered Wagons of Death, so this was a tough call.

Screw it. She was tired, and he was magnificent with his emotions unguarded, his dark eyes snapping, and his cheeks ruddy with anger. Rocking back on her heels, Lucy crossed her arms over her chest and decided to enjoy the unanticipated show. Sebastián had clearly eaten his Wheaties that morning.

His jaw like stone, he glowered at Allie. "So you're telling me you're showing Lucy, your vegetarian friend of over thirty years, your faithful friend who trusted you to find a workable house for her, an option that's above her price range and doesn't feature electricity or running water or a real bed, but does include various terrorized dead animals and the artistic handiwork of a crazed, possibly murderous Oregon Trail enthusiast?"

"Please stop filming," Allie said. "Lucy, I need a word with you in private."

He was having none of it. "No. You're not dragging her off to make her feel guilty for refusing the terrible options you've shown her. She deserves better than that, especially from you. Whatever you need to say, you can say in front of me and the entire crew."

Allie whirled on him. "I suppose talking for her, instead of letting her speak for herself, makes you a better friend?"

Oh, fuck. The cameras were still rolling despite Allie's request, the crew intent on capturing the drama. Both Allie and Sebastián were going to be very, very unhappy if this argument became fodder for national conversation.

And honestly, they were both right. This tiny house option was unacceptable, but Lucy should be the one to articulate that, not Sebastián. Time to stop avoiding the inevitable.

"Enough." Lucy stepped between them. "Allie, let's go outside, as you suggested. Jill, could you please stop filming?"

At Jill's signal, the boom mic operator and the cameraman and camerawoman put down their equipment. They didn't appear happy about it, though.

"Lucy—" Sebastián started to follow the two women outside.

She swung back to him. "No. I can do this myself. Trust me, Seb."

"I do." His mouth tight, he stopped moving. "But I can help."

Unable to resist the impulse, she got on her tippy-toes to give him a grateful kiss. One planted safely on the cheek, of course. No point in revisiting the humiliation of yesterday.

"I need to help myself, I think." She tried to smile. "Soon, you won't be around to protect me."

His jaw worked, and he turned away. "Fine. Call out if you need me."

After she and Allie had walked a good distance from the wagon, she stopped, took a deep breath, and made herself begin a difficult conversation. "I know there aren't a ton of tiny house options on the market right now within my price range, at least none that are already built. But have you seen any other choices? Like a yurt, for example?"

A flush had bloomed on her friend's chest, above the silk of her shell. "We had a plan, Lucy. Why are you making this harder on both of us?"

Lucy shook her head. "I don't know what you mean."

"We talked about this." Allie huffed out a breath. "You'd apply for the show, and I'd be your real estate agent. You'd get to be on TV and spend time with the boy who got away, and I'd take my career to the next level. It's really not that difficult. Or it wasn't, until you *made* it difficult."

Lucy gaped at her friend. How in goddess's name had Allie gotten everything so wrong?

"I didn't choose this experience to get myself on TV. I could take or leave the cameras." She bit her lip. "I didn't apply to spend time with Sebastián, either. I need a house, Allie."

Although, now that she thought back on that initial, wine-soaked conversation about the show, she hadn't agreed to apply until Allie had mentioned Sebastián as someone Lucy could recruit as help. She'd known he wouldn't refuse her, not with such a stressful and important task, no matter how much he prized his privacy.

This show had bought them three full days together. More than they'd had since those endless summers as teenagers. Had that been her subconscious aim all along?

"And I need to support my children in a slow housing market, since their dad's a deadbeat." Allie's hands had clenched into fists. "All you had to do was pretend for three days, maybe four. Help the filming go smoothly, so I could pick up my kids on time. Find nice things to say about each of the options, even if you hated them. Make believe you were considering them. I thought you, of all the Pollyannas in the world, could do that to support me."

The amethyst slid into Lucy's palm, slick and cool. "I'm so sorry."

She was, sincerely. Allie was clearly desperate to make a name for herself and claw her way toward financial stability, and Lucy—selfishly—hadn't considered childcare issues any of the times she'd interrupted filming.

Still, she couldn't afford to playact through the process, for obvious reasons. "I need a house, though. Not as a ploy to snag my high school BFF, but because I'm moving soon. Can't you find me something workable?"

Allie threw her hands in the air. "Do you honestly think I haven't tried? Do you really think I'm such an incompetent real estate agent that I showed you a dilapidated pot shack, the dick bus, and a *covered wagon* because I thought those were *good* options? You have a strict timeline, so you don't want to custom-build something. You have a low budget. I had very little notice before filming began, and I can't produce a perfect tiny house out of thin air, Lucy. I even asked the producers for other options, and they didn't give me any."

Shit. Lucy dropped her chin to her chest, feeling an inch high.

"I sold your condo for above asking price in less than a week." Allie's voice rose. "Can't you just try to play ball, instead of living in some naïve wonderland where you can have exactly what you want without a few compromises? Can't you face reality and *think*, for once?"

A familiar accusation, and one that stung more than it should have.

Lucy gripped the worry stone in her fist and gave herself a minute to return to the present. To consider what her friend —or former friend, as the case might be—had said and whether it rang true even apart from Lucy's own insecurities and doubts.

Deep breaths. In through the nostrils, out through the mouth.

After a few seconds, her pulse no longer thrummed in her ears. Her head cleared. She knew what to say.

"Allie." She spoke quietly. "You're a very good real estate agent, and I'm sorry I didn't consider your position in all this."

Allie dropped her arms to her sides. "Good. So can we just—"

This argument, her old friend's anger, would have gutted Lucy a week ago. But something about the filming process, about these past three days, had allowed her to remember her own needs, to regain confidence in her own judgment.

She couldn't let this conversation derail her now.

"I'm not done." Lucy took another slow, deep breath. "Again, I should have understood your circumstances better, and I apologize. That said, you owe me an apology too."

"What?" Allie's brows drew together. "I—"

"The accusations you just made may or may not be true. Either way, they weren't a kind thing to say to a client and a longtime friend. Also, my supposed naïveté doesn't change any of the crucial facts. I'm not buying this house. I'm not buying *any* of the houses. And I don't plan to lie or mislead property owners on cable television. If that's what you wanted me to do, you should have told me so from the beginning—in clear language—and I'd have refused to apply for the show."

Allie shook her head, arms akimbo. "I thought you understood the situation, Lucy. Any normal person would have."

Lucy wasn't letting herself be sidetracked. Not this time. "You should have let me know you hadn't found workable tiny houses before filming began, but you didn't. Probably because you wanted to prevent me from backing out. And you should have listened instead of ignoring me when I tried to talk to you two days ago. We could have stopped filming then, before we were both put in this position."

Sebastián was standing near the door of the wagon, watching them both. Making sure she was okay. But she was. For the first time since she'd met Jarrod, she really was.

"I don't think I've been unkind about the options you showed me." She refused to break eye contact with Allie, despite the other woman's obvious anger. "I've merely been honest. If you expected anything from me but honesty, you haven't been paying much attention over the past thirty years of our friendship."

After she'd said her piece, she felt lightheaded and unsteady. But Sebastián was suddenly beside her, his hand on her elbow keeping her upright. And she didn't regret anything she'd told Allie. She wouldn't beg for forgiveness or flagellate herself for being who and what she was. Not anymore.

Allie released a breath through her nose. "This is ridiculous."

"Maybe so," Lucy said. "But if you ever speak to me in such an unprofessional way again, consider yourself my former real estate agent."

Turning her head, she caught Jill's eye. "Can we finish filming now?"

"Sure." The woman offered her a thumbs-up from the

wagon's doorway. "You heard her, people. We're in the home stretch!"

Allie brushed past Lucy, but Sebastián stayed put. In fact, he looped an arm around her shoulders and pulled her tight against him, giving her a fierce squeeze.

"You okay?" His voice was low and concerned.

She nodded. "Yes."

"That..." He shook his head a little. "That was magnificent."

"That was long overdue." She drummed up a small smile. "I'm not a huge fan of conflict, as you might have noticed."

He kept looking at her, those dark eyes soft. And he wasn't letting her go. In fact, he hitched her even closer, until they were pressed together front-to-front. Through the thin fabric of her tie-dyed tunic, the heat of his hands seared her back.

"The sparkle is back," he said, confusingly.

She looked down at her top. "That's my other tunic. This one doesn't sparkle."

"Yes, she does." He lowered his mouth for the length of a breath, his lips gentle and warm and seeking against hers. "I can't tell you how glad I am to see it."

She clung to him as he kissed her again. His mouth courted hers, rubbing and nuzzling, until her lips parted beneath his. Then his tongue touched hers for the first time, and in the space of a single moan, a single shudder, the embrace exploded into raw carnality. He was squeezing her ass with one hot hand, cradling her skull with the other as his tongue dueled with hers, twisting and exploring and claiming.

He tasted like the tart apple he'd eaten for breakfast, and he smelled like sea salt and sage and damp skin. Like her friend pushed to the edge of endurance, heated to the point of combustion. She plunged her fingers into his hair, the inky strands a cool contrast to the furnace of his body, and he groaned at the touch of her fingers against his scalp. Sucking her lower lip into his mouth, he nipped it, licked the spot with his tongue, and soothed the sting.

She whimpered, and he shook against her. One of his legs nudged between her thighs, and he bent her backwards, her weight supported by his strength alone.

His cock nudged against her hip, hard with urgent need, and she wanted her hands on it. Her mouth. She wanted to make him come and demand the same in return. Sebastián would make it good. He'd give her what she needed in bed. The time, the effort, the skill. The trust.

She was pressing against his leg, shameless in her desire. Growing swollen and slick and achy from the fierce display of possession and passion, totally unexpected from such a controlled, careful man.

Then he was levering her back to her feet, keeping his hands on her arms until she could stand unsupported. He stepped away, his lips swollen and damp from hers, a furrow between his brows.

She blinked at him, dazed.

Wow. Oh, wow. He'd reached for her. Kissed her. Slid his hand down to her ass and cupped it. Told her she *sparkled*.

She'd considered her hopes foolish, a product of wishful thinking. But maybe those erections of his hadn't been generic, after all. Maybe they'd had a brand name on them. *Her* name, in huge, throbbing, tumescent letters.

And goddess knew, after everything that had happened the last few days, Lucy's vagina might as well have *Sebastián Castillo* emblazoned on it.

She frowned. In it? Along it? Vaginal emblazoning was a linguistically confusing matter.

"You folks ready?" Jill called out from the wagon door.

"I am," Lucy called back. "Ready and willing."

From the heat that flared anew on Sebastián's cheekbones, he knew exactly what she meant.

EIGHT

Lucy knew now. She had to know just how much Sebastián had hidden from her and how long he must have hidden it.

Sure, she hadn't mentioned the kiss since they'd climbed into his car and begun the drive home. But only a fool wouldn't realize the significance of a longtime friend seizing her, bending her over backward, and having her ride his thigh while his mouth devoured hers and his erection prodded her hip. And Lucy might be more innocent than most people, but she was far from a fool.

He'd been so proud of her poise, her willingness to advocate for herself, the renewed confidence shining from her brown eyes. Proud of her and starving for her, the knowledge of their brief remaining time together beating against the inside of his skull like a jackhammer.

Even if a million cameras had been trained on them, he couldn't have stopped himself from reaching for her. If they'd been within a mile of privacy, rather than surrounded by cameras and mics and a television crew, he didn't know whether he could have resisted inching her skirt up her thighs, sliding his hand between her legs, and finding out once and for all what sounds she made when she came. How her sex would quiver and tighten around his fingers. Whether he could push her into a second orgasm with his tongue.

Even with all those onlookers, he'd already learned too much.

Lucy tasted even sweeter than he'd imagined, burned even hotter than he'd dreamed.

How could he go back to pretending? How could he keep acting as if the thought of her imminent departure didn't flay him alive? But how could he bare all his need, all his desperation, after over a decade of concealing both?

Even though she was looking out the window, seemingly unaware of him and his swirling thoughts, she stretched out an arm, and her hand landed on his thigh. He almost drove off the road.

Fuck, he wanted her. More than anything else in his world.

So he'd follow her lead. Let her guide what happened next. But no matter what happened between them, he'd maintain his control. He'd let her go without her knowing how much he wanted her to stay. He'd preserve some small, scared portion of himself.

He'd let her bare her soul, while continuing to hide his.

As he'd always understood, she was so much braver than him.

When they pulled into his garage, he swallowed over a dry throat. "What are your plans for the night?"

Not a statement of his desires. A question, one that might lead her out onto that emotional ledge where he was waiting, although she didn't know it. Would never know it.

New surety glowed in her expression. "The same as yours."

"Ah." He unbuckled his seat belt and fiddled with his garage door opener. Anything to disguise his trembling fingers. "Care to elaborate?"

She freed herself from her own belt. "We have to take care of our four-legged family. Hairy needs a good walk, good food, and a good petting. Kitty probably needs a break from his incessant adoration."

"And then?"

"Then I have to check for work messages. I'm expecting a text or voicemail from that grumpy colonial woman, and I want to get back to her as quickly as possible. I figure you might need to answer a few work messages too."

He inclined his head. "And after that?"

"If we're hungry, we eat."

Food didn't compare to the prospect of her spread naked beneath him. Nothing did.

"And if we're not?"

She traced a line up his leg with a single fingertip, and he let out a shaky breath. This time, she didn't stop at his thigh. Her fingers closed over his jeans-clad erection, her palm providing sweet, teasing pressure, and he wrote lines of code in his head, frantic and struggling to stay in control.

Even in the dimness of the garage, her smile shone. "We figure out whether we're as compatible in bed as we are outside of it."

There. There it was. And he'd earned it without having to commit himself, even once.

But he had to ask. "Is that really what you want?"

"Of course." Her confident smile faded. "Isn't it what you want too?"

He couldn't answer that. Wouldn't. So instead of using words, he reached across the front seat, hauled her into his lap, and kissed her until she'd forgotten her question.

When he let her go, they were both panting.

Rubbing her nose against his, she breathed, "Let's take care of our pets and work."

She climbed off his lap, her hiked-up skirt giving him a glimpse of...something. Something shadowy and wholly unexpected, despite his recent speculation. Holy Jesus, did she really not wear *any* underwear?

He took a moment to gather himself. "Okay."

"Then we can take care of each other." Flicking the skirt down to cover her legs, she smiled again as she headed for the inside of the house.

Like the helpless, lovesick man he was, he followed.

THE TIME HAD ARRIVED, AND SEBASTIÁN'S HEART had twisted itself into a tangled knot. At this point, it was likely as blue and oxygen-starved as his Smurftastic balls.

The pets had been fed, watered, and either petted or given a civilized nod, as Hairy and Kitty respectively preferred. Work messages had been perused and answered. Lucy had decided dinner could wait.

Because they couldn't, she'd said. Not any longer.

She preceded him to his own bedroom, her fingers intertwined with his. She closed the door behind them. And then she let go of him. Without further ado, she grabbed the hem of her tunic with both hands and yanked it over her head. Tossing it onto a table, she put her hands on her hips and let him get an unobstructed view of her breasts for the first time ever.

With her movements, they bounced and settled before his avid gaze. Small. Shaped like teardrops. Crowned by rosy-tan areolas and puckered nipples. Absolutely breathtaking.

He wanted endless minutes to explore the uncharted territory they'd entered. To admire her the way she deserved, the way he'd imagined so many times that week. He wanted to take mental pictures of her just like this, of her magnificent self-possession and the joy crinkling the corners of her eyes as she stood half-naked before him.

He might need those memories to sustain him when she left.

But Lucy didn't seem worried about the future. She also wasn't interested in feigning either patience or shyness. Before he could do more than blink a few times in stunned appreciation of her breasts, she was tugging her skirt down to her ankles and kicking it aside.

Somewhere in the depths of his lust-shrouded brain, he attempted to recall the symptoms of heart attacks. Crushing pressure in his chest? Check. Breathlessness? Definitely. Tingling in unusual places? Oh, yes.

As far as he knew, though, heart attacks didn't cause erections. So he had to assume Lucy, rather than a stoppage in his arteries, was causing his current distress.

With a grin in his direction, she bounded up onto the bed and knelt—completely and utterly naked, holy fuck—in the middle. Then she held out her hands.

"What are you waiting for?" She wiggled her fingers. "Come and get me."

He didn't know the answer to that question. He only knew that whatever she asked of him, he'd do.

As he pulled his tee over his head, he resented the moment she spent out of his sight. But then she was there again, smiling at him as he unzipped and shucked his jeans, then his briefs.

Her gaze fell directly to his dick. "Congratulations on a very successful puberty, Seb."

He had to laugh. "If only my gym classmates could see me now."

"You could always e-mail them or send Facebook DMs.

You have options." She beckoned him forward with a single fingertip. "Still not much hair on your chest, though."

He climbed onto the bed. "I consider it a fair tradeoff."

"Me too, since I find body hair scratchy." She pursed her lips. "I suppose that makes me a hypocrite, doesn't it?"

"No." Shaking his head, he trailed his hand up her thigh. "Just human. Consistency isn't exactly the hallmark of our species."

"True." She shivered under his touch, and he let his fingers drop from her body.

If he followed his instincts, he'd pounce on her, sweep her beneath him, and get his hands and mouth on those sweet breasts at long last. Tell her how perfect he found her curvy legs, her lush hips, and that round ass. Then show her how he could tease those gorgeous nipples until they were stiff and straining for his mouth, how he could make her gasp with a slow, hot circle of his tongue around her clit.

Instead, he waited, his hands fisted at his sides.

She couldn't know how hungry he was for the feel of her against him, skin to skin. But she fed him anyway, with that characteristic generosity of hers, reaching for him and tumbling him beneath her.

She propped her elbows on either side of his head. "Hi, there."

The welcome weight of her pressed him into the mattress, and he wanted to keep sinking, keep descending, until he drowned in softness and Lucy. Until his lungs were suffused with the scent of honey, and the taste of her filled his mouth. Until the world and all his fears disappeared, leaving only her, naked and warm and happy in his arms.

That wasn't going to happen. But her breasts were so close, and he could at least get a fleeting glimpse of what he wanted. He could give her pleasure, even in the midst of disguising the violence of his own need.

So he raised his head and rubbed his cheek against her, letting the incipient stubble on his face prickle against her soft skin, her beaded nipple. Lifting a hand, he cupped the slight weight of her breast and brushed across its tight point with the pad of his thumb. It stiffened further beneath the contact, her areola furling into an intricate, fascinating design.

She squirmed against him, but he didn't hurry. He rubbed and circled until she closed her eyes, swallowing hard. Then he plucked her nipple, pinching lightly. Just hard enough to prick at her nerve endings and stimulate her.

Her hips began a subtle rock against his, and he took her nipple into his mouth and sucked. Her legs opened, and then she was straddling him, her knees planted beside his ribs as she supported herself on her hands and moaned.

He prodded the tight nub of flesh with his tongue and gave her nipple one last, harder suck. Then he moved to the other side, teasing her and licking her until her eyes closed and her hair fell around them both.

After another minute, she murmured, "Enough teasing."

Her weight shifted atop him, and her right hand grasped his cock, her grip firm and knowledgeable. His head fell back, his lips parting. He could only clutch her to him then, only run his hands in frantic strokes along her sides and back, only squeeze her round ass as she took control and pumped him up and down, up and down.

Oh, Jesus. He wasn't going to make it. He was going to explode in her hand before he even got inside her. Certainly before she had a chance to come. But he couldn't seem to move away from the blinding pleasure of her touch.

She claimed his mouth, tracing the seam of his lips with her tongue until he opened to her. Her tongue flicked against his, playing. He sucked the tip of it, and the rhythm of her hand faltered. Encouraged, he did it again, and she arched against him, her grip loosening.

His mind cleared just enough to do the right thing.

Gently, he pulled her hand away from his cock. She was draped over him, her legs on either side of his. The perfect position for what he wanted.

Sliding his hand between their bodies, he stroked over her belly and combed through her curls. Then he reached her wet heat, and his mind went white.

Christ. Christ, she was soft and slippery beneath his fingers. At the first rub of his thumb over her clit, she jerked and made a choked sound.

"Yes," she breathed. "Do that again."

Oh, fuck, he wanted to. He really did. But he had something else in mind.

He parted her folds, opening them. Then he positioned his erection along that wet furrow, took her hips in his hands, and slid her back and forth, letting the pressure and hardness of his cock rub against her clit.

"Ohhhh." Her legs spread further, and she started panting. "That feels…"

He circled his hips, and she bit her lip, bearing down on him.

Her slickness was bathing the base of his cock, she was rocking against him and whimpering, and this was the best sexual experience of his life, bar none. Her entire body stiffened, and she gave a loud, low moan as her sex twitched against his erection and she began shuddering in orgasm.

He couldn't stop himself from coming at the same time, the smell and sounds and feel of her pleasure too much for him to endure.

She collapsed on top of him as he jerked and groaned, his mind mercifully blank.

Recovering a few stray brain cells took a long, long time.

And then they were lying there, trembling and gasping, glued together with various bodily fluids, and he bit his tongue to stop himself from declaring his fealty and his heart. From cuddling her close and swearing he'd never let her go again.

Because he would let her go. Soon. So he had no idea what to say or do. What he *could* say or do without revealing too much.

Mercifully, however, Lucy took charge once again. Tipping up her chin, she planted a kiss on his mouth. After levering himself off of him, she crawled to the edge of the mattress and hopped down.

As she headed for the bathroom with remarkable energy, she called out cheerfully, "One orgasm down, many more to go!"

As always, she was the optimistic sort. But in this case, he thought he could oblige.

NINE

AFTER THEY'D BOTH CLEANED UP, LUCY immediately climbed back on top of the tangled sheets. Sebastián, however, waited by the side of the bed, his thick brows drawn in concern.

Not that her gaze lingered on his brows. Not when such an impressive display of manhood stood before her, completely uncovered and hers to touch.

He wasn't bulky. Instead, he was all sleek lines and lithe muscles. Undeniably fit, with the strong thighs and thick biceps to prove it, but lean. Not a man impressed with muscle size for its own sake. And he had next to no body hair, except under his arms and around the exceptional package Mother Nature had seen fit to give him in recompense for delayed physical development.

Her new favorite feature on his body: the little dimple above each cheek of that taut, round ass. Or maybe the arch of his back when she stroked his cock, or the lines carved across his forehead as he tried to hold back for her sake, or the tight buds of his nipples when he came. She couldn't decide.

His body was just as beautiful as his soul. She'd be able to entertain herself an indefinite length of time by watching him, no matter how long he stood by the bedside and said nothing.

Still, he looked worried.

"Seb..." She sprawled on her stomach, resting her chin on her fists. "Is everything okay?"

He paused, the furrow between his brows smoothing. "Is everything okay for you?"

That wasn't an answer. She shouldn't have been surprised.

Since the moment they'd entered the bedroom, he'd seemed more *hesitant* than she'd expected. She'd have thought maybe he just didn't have much experience, but considering the skills he'd displayed over the past few minutes, she didn't give a lot of credence to that theory.

Maybe he was simply weirded out by the transition from platonic friends to lovers. Or regretting the decision to make that transition?

No. No, she wouldn't question her instincts any longer. Sebastián wanted her. First-time sleepovers always tended toward the awkward. No need to read anything more into it.

"I'm so glad that happened." She grinned at him. "I'd like it to happen again. Like, now."

He didn't respond by sharing his own joy in their newfound intimacy. At least, not verbally. But he moved at long last, leaping into bed and crawling toward her with a glint in his dark gaze she'd never seen before.

Draping himself over her back, he nudged her hair aside and whispered into her ear. "What do you want me to do?"

His resurgent erection prodded her ass, and she wriggled beneath him.

"I want you inside me. But first..." His arms had tunneled under her, and he was sweeping across her nipple with his thumb while his other hand slid between her legs. "Yeah. That." She sighed, her eyes closing. "That feels amazing."

He flipped her over, so she was spread across his bed on her back, and he could touch her more easily as he knelt between her legs. His hand lowered to her curls once more, spreading her open, his thumb circling her clit. When she let out a shaky breath, he slid two fingers inside her. Then three.

Those clever fingers were stretching her wide. Thrusting in and out of her sex, rubbing against the most sensitive spot inside, as she shifted and whimpered and splayed her legs wider.

She cupped her own breasts and pinched her nipples, reveling in the pleasure. No one had ever elicited this kind of easy response from her before, not even the lovers she'd have called good in bed. Something about Sebastián, the way he measured her reactions, the way she trusted him, tipped her over some invisible edge.

"Do you want my mouth too?"

Color high on his cheekbones, he was staring at his slick fingers on her, inside her. His lips had parted, and he was breathing hard. And that magnificent dick was stiff and wet at the tip and begging for attention.

"Do you want my mouth on *you*?" she countered.

He ignored her question. "Answer me."

"Of course I do." She levered herself up on her elbows. "But Seb, I'm—"

He began licking her then, his tongue soft and slow as it circled her clit, while his fingers still rubbed and rubbed inside her. At the sight of his dark head between her thighs, his tongue on her flesh, her elbows gave out beneath her.

He blew on her clit until she trembled. He licked, swirling around her folds until she couldn't hold back a moan. He sucked her clit between those soft lips and flicked it with that talented tongue until she fisted her hands in his silky hair and bucked against him, her sex clamping around his talented, plunging fingers as she cried out.

Then he rolled on the condom, hooked her legs over his arms, and pushed inside her still-pulsing body. Goddess above, the feel of him thick and deep inside her only made her sob harder and raise her hips for more.

His shoulders were bunched as he worked his cock in and out of her with agonizing slowness, his jaw clenched. Confused by his restraint, she stroked his arms as the last throbs of orgasm faded.

"It's okay." She lifted herself enough to kiss his damp, heaving chest. "You can let go."

He gave his head one desperate shake. Did he want her to come again so soon?

So she touched herself, rubbing her oversensitive clit with light pressure as the slide of his cock inside her shifted from a culmination to an enticement. A tease.

But it wasn't quite enough. "I need more to come."

"Okay." He paused, his pulse visibly beating at the side of his neck. "Harder? Faster?"

"Either." She slid her finger over her clit, and felt the edge of pleasure rising within her again. "Maybe both."

He dropped his chin to his chest and took a deep breath. Then he slammed into her, digging her into the mattress, and she moaned. At the end of the stroke, he circled his hips, grinding her fingers against her clit, and reared back to pound into her again. And again, until she gave a strangled cry and came around his demanding cock.

At the first pulse of her body, he groaned, his face tightening as he pumped into her. He let go of her legs, wrapped his arms around her, and gave her his full weight while he shook. She clutched his sweaty back, her eyes closed as she absorbed his pleasure and her own.

The embrace only lasted a minute. Then he carefully

pulled out of her and rolled away, disposing of the condom. To her shock, he didn't immediately return to her side.

He glanced toward the master bathroom. "I need a shower."

His face had turned neutral. But why? From whom—or what—was he hiding?

"Sounds good." Dazed and fuzzy from her orgasms, she tried to smile. "Do you want to have one together?"

"Is that what you want?"

Something was wrong. Maybe he was just tired or hungry or unsure of her response, though, and a good night's sleep, some food, and a little more affection would fix the problem.

She refused to allow anxiety to taint their first time together. Instead, she needed to trust her own instincts. She needed to believe that Sebastián wanted her in his life and bed as much as she wanted to be there.

At long last, she needed to offer him her heart, with faith he'd handle it with care.

But she couldn't do so in words. Not tonight, when he seemed so overwhelmed. Tomorrow, maybe. In the morning, with the light of day illuminating their path forward.

"Sure. Let's shower together." She got out of bed. "No hanky-panky, though. Not this time. My legs are too shaky from the exploits of Mr. Orgasmo for slippery shenanigans."

A small smile lightened his expression. "Mr. Orgasmo?"

"You earned the title." She took his hand, tugging him toward the bathroom. "Enjoy it."

"I'll try," he said.

Sebastián woke the next morning to a smack across his chest.

He squinted at Lucy through one cracked eyelid, confused.

"Sorry. I forgot you were here," she whispered, her sweet face scrunched in apology.

His other eye opened. "So you hit me?"

"Inadvertently. I was half-asleep and forgot where I was, so I reached for my amethyst on the nightstand. Which wasn't actually a nightstand, but your chest. Sorry again." She tugged the sheet up over his shoulders. "Go back to sleep."

Groggy from their late, energetic night, he closed his eyes. But the sigh of the mattress as she slid out of bed, as well as the rustle of clothing—was she getting dressed, or simply retrieving the worry stone from her skirt pocket?—banished his lingering drowsiness.

As did the memory of her naked beside him last night, so loving and so eager for every brush of his hands, his mouth, his cock. Exactly how he'd have envisioned her, if he'd let himself fantasize in any detail about sex with Lucy.

She was magic. The incarnation of warmth and pleasure, all flushed skin and smiles.

He'd let her guide their time in bed. Managed not to reveal more than his body. But even though he'd somehow kept himself under tight restraint the entire night, he'd still seen stars. He'd never experienced that sort of piercing joy before, and likely never would again.

The memory of making love with Lucy would become a spotlight, he already knew. A blindingly bright moment that would cast the rest of his existence into shadows.

Jesus, the power she held over him. No wonder he was so fucking scared.

When he tried to predict what would happen now, only one nausea-inducing answer came to mind. She'd want to talk about what they'd done and what it meant. She'd want to talk about their future.

He couldn't. He wouldn't.

Opening his eyes a bare millimeter, he watched her gather her stone and return to the bed. When she quietly climbed onto the mattress beside him and settled cross-legged against the headboard, then began taking long, steady breaths, one after the other, he relaxed.

Meditating. She was meditating, the amethyst held loosely in her grip.

He was safe, at least for the moment.

Shutting his eyes yet again, he attempted to doze. But after a few minutes of listening to her inhale and exhale, he grew restless and disgusted with himself.

He was not only a coward, but a ridiculous one. A grown man who'd feign sleep in his own bed, rather than face his best friend the morning after she became his lover.

Unless he pretended to nap until she left Marysburg, which she'd probably find somewhat alarming, he had to have a conversation with her sooner or later. Better for it to be on his terms, on a subject of his choosing. Something that would distract her from the fact that they'd woken in the same bed together for the first time in their long relationship.

Okay. He could do this.

He sat up and looped his arms over his knees. "Do you really think that stone helps ease your worries?"

Despite his interruption of her quiet meditation time, she looked at him and smiled. Then she opened her fingers, revealing the amethyst on her palm. "It's not a matter of what I think or don't think. It does ease my worries. I know, because I've experienced the relief."

"But your degree is in kinesiology and health sciences. Data-driven fields. How can you reconcile that with the idea that a stone has special mind-clearing powers?"

He'd kept his tone gentle but interested. An invitation, rather than a challenge, because he didn't want her to interpret his curiosity as disdain.

She didn't bristle at the line of inquiry in any visible way. Instead, she tilted her head, looking pleased and surprised that he'd broached the topic. That he was interested in her thoughts.

He never asked her personal questions. Another way of deflecting any suspicion that he cared too much, hung on her every word, or hungered to know her inside and out.

How had she even tolerated him for so many years?

"I could answer your question a few ways, depending on whether you want the science or my own experiences, or a mixture of both." She thought for a moment. "I could cite studies that show the efficacy of meditation when it comes to various health concerns. I could describe how handling my stone helps me reach a meditative state. I could tell you the stone serves as a reminder, not an active force whisking away my worries. A tool, rather than something powerful in itself. I could argue that we don't have a full understanding of many matters related to physical and emotional health, so rejecting a possible avenue toward wellness would be shortsighted. Or I could discuss the power and ramifications of the placebo effect, and how it can be harnessed to ease pain and improve lives."

Sebastián considered her arguments. "In other words, if you believe it can help, it will help."

"Sometimes. Not always." Her intent gaze pinned him to the bed. "But believing matters more than people think. What you believe influences how you think and how you act, and that can change your reality."

When he started to say something, she held up a hand. "To be clear: I'm not rejecting science. I'd certainly never debate evolution or the efficacy of vaccines or the reality of human-made climate change. But I'm also not going to dismiss things like worry stones as unrealistic and unsupported by scientific data when they're harmless and may actually help people."

"Believing matters," he repeated.

She nodded, rubbing her thumb over the slick surface of the stone. "It does."

A silent minute passed, and he had no idea what to say. The two of them might as well exist on separate planets. In separate galaxies.

Belief had no place in his cosmos. No value. But for her, it was obviously crucial.

She gave a little nod, seemingly to herself. And when she spoke again, her voice was steady. Confident. "For instance, I believe we were always meant to be more than friends." She smiled at him again and scooted closer. "I believe I made a mistake when I accepted that job so quickly after my breakup with Jarrod."

He stopped breathing.

She maintained eye contact, clearly unwilling to flinch from the import of what she was saying. "I believe I should talk to management and see if there's some way I can stay here in Marysburg, close to you."

With those words, Sebastián's brain exploded into chaos, joy and terror detonating within every cell. He sat frozen in bed beside Lucy, completely dumbstruck.

Last night, she'd given more of herself than he'd ever dared to request, and now she was offering him…everything. Absolutely everything.

The woman he loved was telling him she wanted to stay in Marysburg. Wanted a future together. Wanted *him*.

And she was waiting for his response, her eyes bright with hope.

He couldn't utter a word.

She laid a gentle hand on his arm. "Seb?"

Still, no words came. Because he understood both of them too well.

Of course. Of course a woman as brave as Lucy would bare her emotions, her desires, without equivocation or any attempt to shield herself. Of course she wouldn't let the two of them drift into whatever future awaited them, either together or apart, without an honest conversation.

As he'd feared, though, she was guiding this discussion out onto a limb too slender and shaky for his feeble courage. She'd expect him to follow her there. And this time, if he clung to the trunk and let her sway in the wind alone, she'd never beckon to him again.

His mouth felt gritty and dry, as if someone had poured sand down his throat. He was growing dizzy from lack of oxygen. And she was looking at him with such faith and affection, he couldn't seem to think. Couldn't figure out how to handle this situation without risking either himself or the ties that bound them.

He'd need to rely on the instincts honed over years of hiding, then.

Deflect. Avoid direct questions. Shield his vulnerabilities at all costs.

Of those many vulnerabilities, his love for her was the biggest and most terrifying. Always had been. Always would be.

"Staying in Marysburg..." He tried to swallow. "Is that what you want to do?"

"Yes." She didn't hesitate. "But before I make that call, I need to know what *you* want."

There it was. The invitation onto the limb where she waited with such patience, even as it threatened to crack beneath her.

He could join her. He wanted to, with all the love and

hope a foolish boy's heart could hold. But years of torture at school had made him an adult, with an adult understanding of the world and its cruelties. She might not mean to damage him, but she would. The branch beneath them would crack, and they'd both tumble into darkness.

He'd learned his lesson long ago. Reveal vulnerability, reveal emotion, and someone else would exploit it. Would mock and hurt and target the most fragile, hidden parts of him. And if that didn't sound like the friend he'd known for a decade and a half, so be it. He still wasn't exposing his heart to anyone, not even Lucy.

What if she changed her mind? Or laughed and said she was only joking? Or fell in love with another man? Or grew tired of his baggage and his cowardice and left him naked and alone and heartbroken?

A smart man protected himself, even from the woman who owned his soul.

He was clenching the sheet so hard he heard stitches pop.

His voice emerged rough and hoarse. "You should make major work decisions without worrying what other people think or want."

She flinched. But within a moment, her lips had firmed in determination. She wasn't letting the subject go. Wasn't letting him redirect her toward safer ground.

"Usually, yes. But not in this case." She tugged the sheet out of his grip and took his hand. "Before I upend my life to be with you, I need to know how you feel about me."

What could he say? How could he assuage the dawning hurt in her eyes without revealing too much of himself in the process?

His fingers spasmed against hers. "I...I care about you."

"I know th-that." Her voice cracked on the words, and he wanted to die with the shame of it. "But that was true when we were fifteen too. I need to know how you feel now. Whether your emotions have changed over time. Whether they're powerful enough to alter the course of my life."

He sat beside her, still and silent, for a long, long time.

"I don't know what else to tell you," he finally said.

At that, her breath hitched. Hard.

Her gaze dropped to her lap, and he could see her blinking rapidly. Tears. He'd driven her to tears, the woman he'd never, ever wanted to see in pain. His arms were trembling with the need to surround her, to comfort her, to enfold her and keep her close forever.

He wouldn't—couldn't—let himself move an inch. So she fought her tears alone.

She should hate him for that. Knowing her, she probably didn't.

Luckily, he hated himself enough for both of them.

For some reason, she was still holding his hand. In her other palm rested the worry stone, as always. Her thumb circled the smooth surface of the amethyst, around and around, until her breathing evened and the too-bright sheen of her eyes faded.

Then, after one last circle, her fingers turned lax against his, and he knew. It was done.

"Okay." She let go of his hand and patted his knee. "Okay. Don't worry. What happened last night doesn't have to change anything. Let's just consider it a one-time fling between friends."

He didn't protest. Didn't let the anguished howl in his head emerge from his mouth. Didn't reclaim her hand and refuse to relinquish it.

She eased herself from the bed. "I'll be heading out now. I don't think you're needed for filming today, so try to get more sleep if you can."

He'd been looking down at the sheets, self-loathing sour

in his stomach. When she grabbed fresh clothing and began to get dressed, though, he raised his head.

How could he let her leave like this?

"Lucy," he said, "I don't—"

But he didn't know how to fix the problem, not at a price he was able to pay. So he shut his mouth again.

She didn't urge him to finish his thought. Instead, she smoothed a fresh tunic and skirt into place and dropped the worry stone into her pocket. Then she hefted her backpack and caught his eye.

"You've been so generous to let us stay in your house. But I think Hairy and I would do fine in a hotel. I'll pack my things and get him this afternoon, after filming is done." She mustered a weak smile. "Kitty will be vastly relieved."

If she left, she wasn't coming back. Not before the move, not after.

"Lucy…" He licked his lips. "I…"

No. There was nothing to say. Nothing left but logistics and darkness and heartbreak. And maybe a final gesture to show he cared, although not how much.

"I'll feed and walk Hairy this morning. Don't forget your glasses." His voice remained steady, exactly as he'd trained it to do. "They're on the table in the corner."

"Thank you, Seb." She donned her glasses and blew him a final kiss. "Take care."

"Take care," he echoed.

Then she was gone from his bedroom. Gone from his house.

Gone from his future.

TEN

Lucy was pleasantly surprised. After baring her heart and having it summarily crushed by her best friend, disappointing Allie and a cable television crew was proving comparatively nontraumatic.

Jill frowned. "Where's Sebastián?"

"He's already devoted so much time to this search." Lucy manufactured a smile. "And as he rightly points out, this has to be my decision alone."

"He doesn't have"—Jill's fingers drummed against her clipboard—"*feelings* about your situation he'd like to share? Ideas about what you should do, or about options other than the three homes you saw?"

"Nope." As the hair and makeup artist tutted over the redness around Lucy's eyes, Lucy couldn't sustain her façade of good cheer. "He definitely didn't share any feelings."

Over the years, he'd shared so much with her. His time, his effort, his protection. As of last night, even his body. But he couldn't give more. Wouldn't. So she refused to deny the truth any longer: He was a good friend. A good man. Not a good life partner, at least not for her.

She had to trust her judgment. She had to believe she was worth some sort of declaration of emotion, some sort of reassurance her feelings didn't eclipse his.

Maybe Sebastián loved her. Maybe he didn't. Either way, if he couldn't express it, if he couldn't allow himself to be vulnerable and acknowledge how he felt, whatever emotion he possessed wasn't something around which she could shape her life.

She believed. But she couldn't believe alone, not when it came to love.

"I think our viewers will be disappointed not to see the two of you together one final time." Jill still appeared hopeful. "Can you call him and ask him to come?"

Enough. "I'm sorry, but I can't do that. And while I appreciate your concern for the show and for him, I'd rather not discuss this anymore. Thank you, though, Jill."

The producer strode over to talk with the crew while Lucy rubbed her worry stone and got presentable for the camera. Then, almost before she knew it, filming had begun, and she was facing Allie once more.

"First, we saw the Adventurer's Abode, the perfect forest hideaway for someone who wants to live off the grid," Allie said.

And far away from police surveillance, Lucy mentally added.

"You loved the setting, but were concerned about the lack of separate toilet facilities and the compact size of the loft."

More real estate code: By compact, *you mean absurdly small.*

"Then we looked at the Old-School Sanctuary, where you appreciated the kitchen and bathroom facilities, as well as the abundance of outsider art—"

Dicks. Dicks dicks dicks dicks dicks.

"—and the convenience of a first-floor bedroom."

No. Don't think about cuddling with Sebastián in that bedroom.

"But you were troubled by the prospect of updating the bus to create a clean, modern home."

The operative word being clean.

"Finally, we toured the Pioneer's Pad. Although you admired…" Allie paused, clearly trying to come up with something plausible. "Although you admired the *historical authenticity* of the design, you weren't sure you'd be satisfied without running water or electricity."

Or with the knowledge that the previous owner might have eaten other pioneers.

"So what have you concluded?" Allie looked at Lucy, her gaze pleading. "Which of those properties will be your new home?"

She wanted Lucy to lie. To choose one of the houses, even if she never intended to go through with the sale. And maybe she would have done that a month ago. But articulating her needs had strengthened her. Time and distance from her breakup with Jarrod had strengthened her. Sebastián's support had strengthened her. Most of all, renewed belief in herself and her own judgment had strengthened her.

"I need to thank you, Allie." She deposited her worry stone in her pocket and squared her shoulders. "You worked hard to find me tiny house options in my price range, and you more than demonstrated your excellent real estate agent skills by selling my condo in a tough market in less than a week."

The other woman pursed her lips. She knew what was coming.

"I wish I'd seen something I loved without reservations," Lucy said. "But I can't buy any of the three houses. I'm sorry."

Allie's face drooped. "Are you certain?"

Only a few more minutes, and this ordeal would be done.

"I'm afraid so. I know you devoted a lot of time and effort to this house hunt, and I appreciate both."

A couple more inconsequential exchanges, and then filming finished. Allie didn't say another word to her, just went to talk to the boom mic guy.

A friendship of over thirty years, over. But nothing that had happened during filming could erase those campfires and sleepovers and walks home from the school bus. And even close friendships sometimes faltered, either slowly or in a sudden rupture.

The past few days had taught her that too. Especially the last twenty-four hours.

"I'm sorry this didn't work out for you." Jill's gray brows had drawn together. "We were all hoping you could make a go of it."

"Me too." She shook the producer's hand. "But onward and upward."

Behind her, she could hear the cameraman and camerawoman chatting by the craft services table, soon joined by the hair and makeup artist.

"This is why our other shows feature people who've already bought one of the properties. Stupid demand for authenticity." The camerawoman sounded like she was chewing something. "At least we got good footage the other days."

The cameraman grunted in agreement. "Although you know we're going to get a shitload of letters. We're leaving people with virtual blue balls."

What in the world?

"Lucy, one final heads-up for you and Sebastián." Jill tapped Lucy's arm, drawing her attention away from the crew's conversation. "We may have captured more on camera than you realize. As your release states, we're allowed to use any of that footage in the final show."

Whatever. She wasn't ashamed of a single thing she'd done, on or off camera, international audience or no international audience. Sebastián might feel differently, but he'd signed the release too, and he was a grown man. They could both deal with the consequences of their decisions.

"That's fine," she told Jill. "Do what you need to do. If you got any footage of my argument with Allie, though, I'd be grateful if you didn't use it. Same with the footage of her argument with Seb. She's a great real estate agent, and I want to make sure her talents are presented in the best possible light to viewers at home."

After a few moments of thought, the producer heaved a gusty sigh. "Fine. Even without agent-client throwdowns, I think we have enough drama for this episode."

"Thank you." Lucy gave Jill a heartfelt hug. "I really appreciate all your kindness."

Finally, with a last wave to the producer and the rest of the crew, she headed for her car.

Onward and upward, right? Time to pack her belongings, grab Hairy, and check into her hotel again. For the first time since they'd met, she was kind of hoping she wouldn't have to see or talk to Sebastián along the way.

They might still be friends, but even friends required some emotional distance at times.

Sebastián absented himself from the house for the rest of the day, until he was certain Lucy had come and gone. His desperation to see her one last time, to look into those soft brown eyes and bask in her sweet smile, hadn't waned. But after a few quiet hours alone, his panic and determination to protect himself had.

If he spent another minute in her presence, he might

reveal everything to her. How much he'd always loved her. How that love had transformed over the years, shifting until he could no longer call it platonic, until no other woman in his life and bed would do. How badly he wanted—needed—her to stay by his side.

So instead of waiting at home for her to return, he went to work and began tinkering with his latest model. Which was a better use of his time anyway, since he was running behind after taking several days of vacation.

His coworkers greeted him with casual unconcern, none of them appearing particularly interested in where he'd been all week. Not even Gwen. Probably because he never told her anything personal, even when she asked.

They knew his name. They knew he was an efficient, pleasant coworker. But they didn't know *him*. Not really. His parents and family did, of course. The only other person who'd ever come close was—

Nope. Back to inputting lines of code.

He couldn't believe how quickly and completely his standoffish cat had become accustomed to Hairy's undying affection. When Sebastián had ventured into the kitchen after Lucy's departure, eyes bleary with fatigue and—

Well, that didn't matter. When he'd ventured into the kitchen, he'd found the two pets resting entwined around one another. That Hairy liked to sleep cuddling didn't surprise him. But Kitty, of all creatures? The cat who only deigned to let Sebastián pet her once a year, on his birthday?

When the two animals had woken at the sound of food in their bowls, Kitty hadn't hissed or clawed at Hairy. Instead, she'd butted her head under his chin until he licked her a few times. Then, in her inimitable style, she'd flicked him with her tail and presented him with her ass as she stalked to the litter box.

Hairy hadn't seemed to mind. He'd just stared after her

with his stupid doggy heart in his eyes, as if he and an entirely different species of animal could ever make a go of it.

Those animals were going to miss one another. Almost as much as—

Fuck. He needed to concentrate on his model. If he made one small mistake, the simulation would crash when he tried to run it. His work required the ability to shut out all distractions, to focus on nothing but the job at hand.

Still, he hoped Lucy hadn't listened to Allie. Hadn't let the other woman convince her to choose one of those horrific tiny house options on camera.

He understood his best friend. If she picked a house on cable television, she'd feel obliged to go through with the purchase. The last thing she needed was either a deep-woods pot shack, a dick-festooned bus, or an Oregon Trail enthusiast's fever dream.

If he'd been there to offer support, maybe she—

MATLAB. Focus on MATLAB.

His fingers paused on the keyboard. What she and Hairy really needed was a yurt. Unlike the other tiny houses she'd toured, a yurt would give her plenty of overhead clearance—more than enough to stave off claustrophobia. Lots of options for a client changing area and a decent bathroom. Room for Hairy to run around and torment hapless, aloof cats. She could design the yurt to whatever specifications she wanted, take it down and transport it with relative ease, and pay someone to set it up for her again.

An engineer should be able to look at yurt plans and figure out how best to meet her needs. After all, she expressed them so damn easily, with such faith that they wouldn't be used against her. And when they *were* used against her, as with Fuckhead Jarrod or Allie, she managed to pick up the pieces and regain her confidence somehow. To keep believing that reaching out, holding on, was worth the pain and effort.

Believing matters, she'd said.

A little light Googling wouldn't hurt anyone. After all, he'd originally intended to take more vacation time today, and he wouldn't charge the company for the hours he spent researching yurt options and plans.

What sort of weather conditions could a yurt withstand? Were different types of yurt materials more conducive to different settings? How much would it cost to transport the whole yurt contraption? What sort of supports were needed to create separate spaces within the yurt structure?

He'd never, not once in his life, used the word *yurt* so often. It had lost all meaning to him at this point. Yurt yurt yurt yurt yurt.

Yup. Total nonsense.

An hour or so later, however, he had some yurt-related answers. Given a few days, he suspected he could help design one that would incorporate everything Lucy required and suit her aesthetic sensibilities. Maybe even design two, depending on the decisions she reached about her future.

But still he sat in front of his monitor, hands on the keyboard, frozen in indecision.

The limerick came to him without his volition.

There once was a man so lonely and tired
Who wouldn't reach out for a love that inspired
He lay alone in his room
Filled with such sadness and gloom
Never knowing in his past he was mired.

Not his finest effort. The rhythm in the last line was off. But maybe the sentiment was worth considering anyway.

A few minutes later, he knocked on his boss's office door.

"Come in!" Brent yelled.

Sebastián walked inside and closed the door behind him.

"I thought I wouldn't need the rest of my vacation, but I do. Maybe a few days next week, too. Is that doable?"

"Will you be able to finish your projects before deadline?" His boss didn't look up from the paperwork on his desk. "Because if the answer is yes, take some more time. The office should survive without you."

Especially since Sebastián had ensured his presence there didn't leave much of a mark, except when it came to work-related issues.

"The deadlines won't be a problem," he said. "I'll make the necessary changes to my time sheet."

"Then you're set."

That seemed to be the end of the conversation. "Thanks."

Just as Sebastián turned to leave, however, Brent raised his head from his work. "You never take vacation days. Is everything all right? Is your family okay?"

Normally, Sebastián would end this line of questioning without hesitation. Say he was fine and close his boss's door behind him. And he still didn't plan to parade his private concerns and emotions in front of his coworkers in what was intended to be a professional setting.

But Brent was a good boss and a decent man. Maybe he could be trusted with a little corner of his employee's life.

Sebastián looked at the ceiling for a moment, his jaw clenched. Then he forced out the words. "I screwed things up with someone important to me. I want to fix the situation, if I can."

Brent's fingers stopped tapping his desk, and his brows rose. It was the first piece of personal information Sebastián had voluntarily revealed since his job interview last year, and he suspected the significance wasn't lost on his boss.

"I'm sorry to hear that." Brent sat back in his chair. "Take as much time as you want. If there's anything you need from us in the meantime, just e-mail or call."

"Thanks again. I will." He reached for the door handle.

"Sebastián?" Brent's face had softened, his expression turning sympathetic and warm. "It'll work out."

Sebastián wasn't so sure. But he nodded anyway.

Believing matters.

ELEVEN

Sebastián sent the text a week later, the afternoon before Lucy planned to leave Marysburg for a vacation and then her new job. *Can we meet at my house tonight, after you finish seeing your super-cranky final client?*

She responded within moments, as always. The woman was completely incapable of playing it cool or feigning disinterest.

Sure, she wrote. *I'd already planned to stop by. I have a little something to give you before I head cross-country.*

Since she'd moved back into the hotel, they'd stayed in contact through occasional e-mails and texts, but they hadn't seen each other. Except for one awkward lunch, where she'd smiled a bit too brightly and he'd weighed his every word way too long before speaking.

Tonight should resolve that awkwardness and uncertainty one way or another.

He tapped out his response. *See you at seven?*

Sounds perfect!

The rest of the afternoon passed in a blur of anxiety, as he checked the paperwork for the billionth time and readied his house for Lucy's arrival. But then her Prius was pulling into his driveway, and she was climbing out of her car with a package in her hands, and he was going to lose his fucking mind if he hadn't done so already.

He opened the door before she could ring the buzzer. "Hi, Lucy."

"Hey, Seb." She tilted her head, eyeing him with curiosity. "Are you okay? You look…I don't know. Are you sick?"

"Nope." With a hand at the small of her back, he ushered her inside his home. "Not sick. Happy you're here."

"Wow." The furrows in her forehead deepened before she suddenly laughed. "You're just saying that because I'm leaving soon."

Had he really never told her he was glad to see her? Jesus.

"I'm saying that because it's true." He glanced toward the kitchen. "Do you want a drink? I have some—"

"Thanks, but I can't stay long." She chose to sit on the armchair instead of the couch, the package in her lap. "I just wanted to give you this and say"—she cleared her throat, looking down at the sparkly ribbon on the rectangular box —"goodbye."

From all signs, she wouldn't receive what he wanted to say, the gifts he planned to offer her in return, as well as he'd hoped. But even at her most frustrated and hurt, Lucy Finch wouldn't crush him underfoot. She wouldn't do anything to him he hadn't already done to her for years.

Only a few days ago, she'd offered to stay here in Marysburg for and with him.

He had to believe. In her. In them.

"I have something for you too." Instead of taking the couch, which sat perpendicular to her and way too far away for his liking, he perched on the coffee table facing her. "Do you want to open your gift first?"

She shook her head and handed him the gaily wrapped package. "You go."

The ribbon exploded into a profusion of joyful curls in the center. Not one of them was identical. Handmade, then. She'd carefully folded the edges of the paper and smoothed down the tape until it became invisible.

He opened the gift with care, loath to rip the thick wrapping. Finally, the folds of the tie-dyed paper separated, and he was looking down at himself. Or, to be precise, himself and Lucy. The two of them were lying on a small bed, staring at the ceiling, their heads close together. She was resting closest to the camera and giggling, her smile wide and bright, her nose stud glinting in the light from the bus windows. His face was largely in shadow, his amusement only revealed through the tucked corners of his mouth.

"The dick-lover's Sistine Chapel. Our first sight of it is well worth commemorating." He held the framed photo with care, as if it might sift through his fingers and disappear. "Did the film crew get you a still frame from their footage?"

She nodded. "Your house..." Biting her lip, she paused. "I thought you might like something joyful in your house. Something to remind you that you have a friend who cares about you and wants your happiness. Always and forever."

She rushed on before he could respond. "If you don't want anyone to see it, put it in your bedroom." Her cheeks pinkened. "Although I suppose that's a naïve thing to say. Of course you'll eventually have someone else in your—"

"Lucy." He put down the photo and took her hands in his. "Thank you. I love it."

Her fingers were trembling, and her eyes had turned bright. She was trying so hard not to cry, and his long-ignored heart cracked in his chest.

"I know just the spot for the picture." Standing, he tugged her up beside him. "Let's go and nail it in place."

"Really?" She blinked hard. "You're going to put it up?"

"Yes. Right now." He held one of her hands all the way to his bedroom. "I'm thinking it should go to the left of the bed. There isn't a lot of space on the other walls."

Her brows pinched. "Not enough space? Your room looks like the cell of an antisocial monk who really loves pillow top mattresses."

"See for yourself." He waved her in front of him, gripping the picture frame with unsteady fingers as she walked inside.

Her gasp echoed in his ears.

Mouth open, she drifted to the nearest wall and touched the framed image there. "You and your family at your sister's wedding. What a beautiful photo." Her gaze drifted. "And your parents' house. Was this taken back when we were in high school?"

He nodded. "I'm glad my parents moved someplace nicer, but I still think about that house. I always felt more comfortable there than I did anywhere else." After a pause, he forced himself to keep talking, keep exposing himself. "When I was in college, I'd drive five hours each way to come back on weekends."

"Because you missed the house?"

"Because I missed my family." He swallowed. "A lot."

"I didn't know that." Her voice was hushed, as if she feared disturbing whatever was occurring in this room. Whatever had changed between the last time she'd seen his bedroom and now.

He braced himself. She hadn't spotted the most revealing decorations yet, but she was moving closer.

"Is this picture..." She swiveled to face him. "Is this the creek where we used to go after school and during the summers?"

"The Marysburg stream. My favorite place in the world." He gazed at the grass, the sparkling water in the photo.

Anything not to meet her eyes. "I think about you every time I see it. I think about sitting with you by the water every time I need to calm and comfort myself."

"I had no clue. None." A twinge of hurt sounded in her voice, but also wonder.

Then she reached the wall near the bed. Even if he hadn't been watching her progress, he'd have known where she was from the sudden silence.

"Lucy..." He trailed off, unsure what to say.

She touched a gilded frame. "You kept my senior pictures all these years."

"You had bangs back then." Embarrassed and exposed, he lifted a shoulder. "It was cute."

"How..." Slowly, she turned in place, scanning all the walls of the room. "How did you get all these photos of the two of us?"

"My parents took some when we weren't looking. I asked them for copies." He let out a slow breath. Might as well tell her all of it. "There were a couple of us from the back of the yearbook. I scanned those."

She wandered to the left of the bed and sucked in another harsh breath. "Oh, my goddess."

"The crew must have rolled their eyes at us. But they gave me a still frame from their footage without telling me you'd done the same thing." Forcing his legs to move, he stepped next to her. "Holding you, having you beneath me, made that horrible, claustrophobic loft the most wonderful place I'd ever been."

He'd positioned the photo next to his bed for good reason. The way her heavy-lidded gaze met his, the ease with which she cradled his body between her legs, the possessive claim of his hands in her hair, the parting of her lips...

It incinerated him. Every time.

She blinked, her brow creased. "You almost smushed your

brain in that loft. Like, two seconds after the picture must have been taken."

"Holding you was worth every lost bit of gray matter." Despite his anxiety, he couldn't help but smile. "Which isn't to say I wanted you to buy the Pot Palace."

"Don't worry. I didn't."

The words sounded absent. She was working through what she was seeing and hearing, testing out the implications and reaching conclusions.

"That's what the crew said." He'd known in his heart she would stand her ground, but he was glad anyway.

"Seb, what does this m—"

He laid the frame on his bed and strode for the door, lightheaded from the rapid beat of his heart. "Let's put your picture on the wall later. You should take a look at my gift before we talk more."

The rolled sheaf of papers was lying on the kitchen island, tied together with a satin ribbon. Rainbow-colored, her favorite.

After he handed it to her, everything in his body seemed to freeze in place. He couldn't move, couldn't speak, couldn't think. He could only watch her unroll his heart, which he'd offered her in schematic form. He was an engineer, after all.

She scanned the top blueprint first. "You..." Her head gave a little shake. "You found designs for a yurt? I don't... I don't understand."

His paralyzed vocal cords finally unfroze a fraction. "I want you to have everything you need in your new home. Everything that would make your life easier and happier. I couldn't find one yurt design that encompassed all the necessary features, so I combined a couple of different plans. Then I ran them by the custom-built-yurt company to make sure they were feasible." He rolled his eyes. "And then I ran them by an architect and a structural engineer too, because I think those yurt people were high when I talked to them. I wanted to make sure you'd be warm, safe, and able to transport the yurt easily."

When she looked up at him, her eyes were wet again. Not with happiness. Her mouth was trembling, her cheeks pale. And although he hated every moment of her pain, although he wanted to haul her into his arms and dry her tears, he couldn't help but consider her distress a good sign.

Despite those tears, she tried to smile. "This is so kind of you."

"Anything for you." He licked his lips. "The build will come in below budget, by the way. You can also use sustainable materials, since that's important to you. I know you could have done all this yourself, but I wanted to make things easier for you. A new home and a new job are a huge transition."

"I thought—" She cut herself off, blinking hard. "Never mind. It doesn't matter what I thought. This is such a lovely gift, Seb. Thank you." Flipping through the other papers, she frowned. "Are these additional views of the design? Or blown-up details from it?"

Here it was. The moment that would either save him or leave him a hollow wreck of a man forever.

"That's a different design." Jesus, why was his throat so dry? "Um… in case you need something else."

"Something else?" She spread out the second set of plans on the island, holding down the edges with her hands. "I don't…"

When she didn't finish her sentence, he made himself ask. "You don't what?"

"I'm not sure I understand these plans." She squinted at them, scanning from left to right, top to bottom. "There's no kitchen. No real bedroom, either. And what's this little area for?"

Her finger tapped a room set off from the rest of the yurt.

"A changing room." Oh, shit, he couldn't swallow. "For clients. And there's space for a little refrigerator with bottled water, along with lots of storage for all your supplies and tables. No need for a kitchen or bedroom, not in your place of business."

She raised her head, face blank. "You designed me a massage yurt?"

Why couldn't he remember the speech he'd memorized so carefully? "Uh…yeah."

"But I'll be working for Massage Mania. I won't need a separate space."

She'd misunderstood. Which meant, God help him, he'd have to explain.

"I want you to have a choice." The words emerged in a rush, a flood contained behind a dam of fear for too long. "Because yes, my heart will crumble to pieces if you leave. But you're my friend, as well as the woman I love. I want you to be happy more than I want you to be with me. So if you decide your future is out west, take the first set of plans. Be safe and warm and happy in your tiny yurt home. But if you decide your future is here, in Marysburg, with me…take the second set of plans."

Those soft brown eyes had widened in shock. "Did you just say you lo—"

But he couldn't let her interject. He had to get it all out now, before his courage failed him.

"Take the second set of plans," he repeated. "Open your own business. Build that massage yurt in my backyard, where there's more than enough room. I've already researched the permits we'd need. Live with me." His voice cracked. "W-work there, and live with me. Fill my house with joy and love and everything else that makes you remarkable."

When he finally stopped speaking, a deathly silence fell over his house.

She stared up at him, wordless, her expression so full of conflicting emotions he couldn't read it.

In sheer kneejerk defensiveness, he almost took it all back. Almost laughed and said he was joking, he'd just wanted her to have as many yurt options as possible, haha, how funny. Of course he didn't love her. Of course he didn't need her like the tides needed the moon, like a man lost in the vastness of space needed oxygen and warmth.

But believing mattered. Above all else, *she* mattered. More than his pride or the fears that gripped him so tightly sometimes he couldn't breathe.

"Please," he whispered. "Please, Lucy. Stay with me."

Nothing. Not a word. Not a movement.

"I know I need help, and I'll get it. I'll find someone to talk to. I swear." He bowed his head. "Please, just give me a chance to show you everything I've been hiding for too long."

Slow tears were dripping down the sides of her beloved face. Tears born of joy? Of sadness that she was leaving him heartbroken?

"The last page is a limerick." He thrust it in front of her with a shaking hand. "For you."

There once was a man who adored you
He waited and waited and scored you
Now he's lost for a path
Because none of his math
Will express all his feelings toward you.

She gave a huge sniff. "Scored me? Classy, Seb."

"I did my best." With an impatient hand, he knuckled aside the wetness under his own eyes. "I'll always do my best for you. I know I fucked up last week, but I promise nothing like that will ever happen again. Although it may take me some time to learn how to—"

"Open up?" At his nod, she pushed aside the limerick with a decisive gesture. "So, if I understand you correctly, your plan is for me to quit my job before I begin, build a massage yurt in your backyard, and start an entirely new business."

"And live with me." He brushed away her tears with his thumbs. "That's the most important bit."

She looked him straight in the eye. "Is that what you want?"

It was a deliberate echo, he knew. Of every time he'd asked her that question instead of telling her what he was thinking. Of every time he'd required her to climb out onto an emotional limb and sway in the wind while he clung to the tree trunk.

This time, he was taking the risk too. Because at long last, he finally believed.

"Yes." No hesitation. No doubt. "That's what I want."

That unreadable expression, so unfamiliar on her face, transformed into the most beatific smile he'd ever witnessed. And he'd seen thousands of her smiles. Maybe millions. All of them beautiful, all of them joyful. But none filled with such incandescent pride and elation and love.

Because she did love him. He believed that too.

She flung herself into his arms, knocking them both against the island. He found her mouth, those trembling lips he loved, and pressed a kiss there. Another. Another.

It felt right, like nothing else in his life ever had.

"I love you," she told him between kisses.

He smiled against her mouth. "I know."

EPILOGUE

Cowan opened the new message in his inbox, noting three photo attachments. "I think Lucy Finch got back to us with pictures from her engagement party."

"Finally." Irene swiveled away from her monitor and focused on his. "Hippies have no sense of urgency."

Over the past few weeks, he'd grown rather fond of Ms. Finch and Mr. Castillo. Their episode was likely to become a viewer favorite, as well as HATV's only episode of Tiny House Trackers that could be considered erotically charged, due to footage the couple hadn't noticed the cameras capturing.

"The party only happened three days ago," Cowan said. "Cut her some slack."

Irene couldn't abide delays or obstacles thwarting her progress, which made her a fearsome HATV intern but an exhausting coworker. And although he would never admit it to her, also a very stimulating—but frustrating—companion.

"The episode airs next week, and we'll need to add those photos to the follow-up segment at the end." The crease of her brow, barely visible under her heavy black fringe of bangs, indicated her concentration as she tapped out a message to the Tiny House Trackers staff. "I hope there's time."

"Should be. Don't worry." After reading the lovely, seemingly sincere letter of thanks Ms. Finch had written to accompany the pictures, he clicked through the images. "Oh, wow."

Irene's gaze focused again on his monitor. "Wow indeed. It pains me to say this, but the tie-dyed dress looks good on her. Someone needs to talk to her about frizz control products, though."

He shook his head. "Not that. Look at Mr. Castillo's expression."

Clad in a crisp white shirt, subtly patterned tie, and dark suit, the man was standing among a group of conservatively clad people with dark hair and golden-brown skin, along with a number of pasty-white folks sporting ponytails and Jimi Hendrix tees and throwing peace signs.

Cowan figured he could work out which family was whose.

Mr. Castillo had wrapped his arms around Ms. Finch from behind, his chin propped on her shoulder. He was beaming, his lean face creased in joy.

"What's so weird about his expression?" Irene squinted and leaned closer to the monitor. "He looks like a normal, happily engaged man to me. Maybe hotter than the average prospective bridegroom, but that's the only difference I can see."

Smothering a foolish flare of irritation, Cowan spread his hands. "Exactly. Remember all those complaints from Jill about how he never showed any emotion? Before she caught the secret footage, she thought he and Ms. Finch were platonic friends."

Irene tapped her stylus along the edge of her tablet. "I

remember him being hard to read during his intake interview."

Was that her type? Stoic and stone-faced?

Whatever. Mr. Castillo was taken, whether or not he fulfilled Irene's no-doubt numerous and arcane requirements for male companionship.

"He was very hard to read. But in these pictures, he looks completely transformed." Cowan clicked on the next photo. "This is a great shot of the two of them."

Lucy Finch was looking directly into the camera, her nose wrinkled under those tortoiseshell glasses as she laughed. None of the hesitance and anxiety he'd seen in her intake interview showed in the picture. No doubts. Just effervescent happiness as she leaned against her fiancé's chest, snuggling close.

For Mr. Castillo, though, the camera might as well have disappeared. He didn't pay it any attention. Instead, he was watching the face of his friend, his new fiancée, with the sort of rapt attention and adoration that tightened Cowan's chest.

He wanted that. Not soon, but someday.

Maybe it would be easier to find if he weren't working eighty hours or more per week, or if he spent significant time around any woman other than Irene.

"Did she send a picture of her massage yurt too?" Irene paused. "That may well be the most ridiculous phrase I've ever uttered in these studios, which is saying something."

He checked the third photo. "Yup."

More tapping on Irene's tablet. "I'll make sure all three pics make it into the episode, along with some bullshit about true love, happily ever after, blah blah blah."

Swiveling to face her, he tilted his head. "You don't believe in true love?"

"You do?" Her red-painted upper lip curled. "More time

spent working with Break Up/Shake Up should cure you of that."

The show about post-divorce home renovations boasted notoriously bitter applicants. Intake interviews often consisted entirely of obscenity-laden rants about exes, interspersed with fervent paeans to quartz countertops and shiplap.

Again: Whatever. Irene's misguided beliefs about love didn't matter. His job did.

He forwarded Ms. Finch's e-mail to the appropriate parties. "What's next on the agenda?"

"I just got a message from the producer of Flipping Foul Play." She read it aloud. *"Flipper Kate wants to plan a surprise proposal for the next live episode. Apparently, she and Flipper Nick have been carrying on a secret relationship where the cameras couldn't see them, and she wants to take it to the next level. I need your help."*

Cowan sat back, crossing his right ankle over the opposite knee. "How is a secret relationship even possible? The cameras are rolling all the time on that show."

Irene just shrugged.

"And I thought those two loathed one another."

Like, sincerely loathed. Especially after Flipper Nick's sabotage had cost Flipper Kate the last challenge and that bonus ten-thousand-dollar prize. Not that Cowan followed the show religiously or anything.

His coworker laughed. "Loathing doesn't preclude a few late-night hate fucks, kid. Anyway, Deena is pretty excited about the proposal idea, since it should bring in huge ratings."

As befitted a full-grown man, Cowan ignored Irene's continued use of the word *kid*. "So what does she want us to do?"

"Go through this season's footage and find any evidence of the secret romance, so the editors can piece things together for viewers." Irene's shoulders acquired an uncharacteristic droop. "*All* this season's footage, up to the previous episode."

"But…" He gave his head a frantic shake. "There are so many cameras on that show. The sheer volume of footage—"

"I know. Hope you wore comfy clothes, Cowan." Despite the exhaustion painting dark shadows beneath those sharp green eyes, Irene managed to direct an evil grin his way. "Because we're going to be here a loooooong time."

Not only that night, but the next few evenings too. Well, shit. So much for his half-baked plan to hit some local bars and talk to a few women. Ones who didn't call him *kid* and consider him a wet-behind-the-ears rube, despite many productive weeks of working together.

"I'll order the pizza." She tapped the number on her phone's contacts list. "You pay."

Cowan sighed and fished his credit card from his wallet. "Your wish is my command, your highness."

"Damn right," Irene said. "All hail the HBIC of HATV."

THE END

THANK YOU FOR READING *TINY HOUSE, BIG LOVE*. ♥ I hope you enjoyed Lucy and Seb's story! Please consider leaving a brief review where you got this book. Reviews help new readers figure out if a book is worth reading!

If you would like to stay in touch and hear about future new releases in this series or any of my other series, sign up for the Hussy Herald, my newsletter: https://go.oliviadade.com/Newsletter

And turn the page for a list of my other books and a suggestion on what to read next!

ALSO BY OLIVIA DADE

LOVESTRUCK LIBRARIANS

Broken Resolutions

My Reckless Valentine

Mayday

Ready to Fall

Driven to Distraction

Hidden Hearts

THERE'S SOMETHING ABOUT MARYSBURG

Teach Me

Cover Me / Work of Heart

LOVE UNSCRIPTED

Desire and the Deep Blue Sea

Tiny House, Big Love

PREVIEW OF COVER ME

CHAPTER 1

THE HOSPITAL GOWN DIDN'T FIT.

Elizabeth tugged at the edges in front, but all that did was pinch her armpits. The worn, thin material couldn't stretch any more. It would tear if she yanked harder. And the young woman who'd led the way to the curtained dressing booths had said to leave the gown open in front, so Elizabeth couldn't reverse the garment.

The jeans covered some of her, but not enough.

She didn't dare look at herself in the mirror. No need to see her breasts and upper belly spilling through the opening, the flesh pale and pebbled by the chill of the Marysburg hospital.

Any other time, the embarrassment and discomfort might have brought stinging color to her cheeks, even though over four decades of life as a plus-size woman and many visits to this very hospital—and its very inadequate gowns—should have inured her to such indignities. But today, no. She wouldn't pray the hospital would invest in bigger gowns or wonder what those spotting her would think about her weight.

Marysburg General was offering free mammograms today, or at least cooperating with the local breast cancer awareness organization who'd advertised the event. That was good enough for her, even if she had to parade down the antiseptic-scented hallways half-naked.

She didn't know who was really paying for the mammograms, the hospital or the organization. She didn't care. The money wasn't coming from her depleted checking account, and the results from today should relieve weeks of fear.

So she simply held her sweater in front of the gap in her gown, covering all the crucial bits, and drew back the curtain with a metallic rattle. The tech who'd led her to the dressing room was working at a nearby computer, her dark brows knitted.

She looked up after a moment, then winced when she saw Elizabeth's predicament. "I'm sorry." Her ponytail swished as she shook her head. "We've been so busy today, I forgot to get you the right type of gown. If you want to go back into your dressing room, I can bring you one."

No. Elizabeth couldn't wait another moment.

"It's fine." She glanced at the name on the woman's badge, her cheeks aching from a forced smile. "Thank you for the offer, Cailyn. But I figure I'm supposed to be flashing the goods soon anyway, right?"

Cailyn's shoulders relaxed. "True enough. And the room is just down the hall. Follow me."

They proceeded past several doorways and the bustling nurses' station before entering the room with the mammogram machine. It looked newish, shiny and clean, although Elizabeth knew she couldn't expect 3D images from it. Not when someone else was paying.

The machine. The chairs. The table. Everything in this space was familiar. Nothing had changed since last year's mammogram, other than her insurance status.

And one other terrifying, crucial detail.

Despite the coolness of the hospital, slick perspiration had gathered under her arms. Deodorant could throw off mammograms, of course, so she hadn't used any that morning. She suspected she'd have been sweating either way, though.

"Um…" She licked her lips and tasted blood. The dry air of late winter always caused chapping if she wasn't careful, and she hadn't been paying much attention to anything outside her own head in recent days. "You might want to look closely at my right breast."

Cailyn paused in her adjustment of the machine. "All right."

"In the shower last month, I found a—" She faltered, then made herself finish. "I found a lump along the side. Toward the middle. You can't see it, but it's pretty easy to feel. I think it's a cyst, since I tend to get those, but I don't know. It doesn't hurt."

"Hmm." Cailyn crossed the room and flipped through Elizabeth's various registration forms. "Have you discussed this issue with a primary care physician? Especially given your family history and risk factors?"

Her time as a smoker in her twenties. Her grandmothers. The fact she'd never been pregnant. All things she'd noted on those forms. All things she'd been unable to forget since she'd slicked Ivory soap over her breast and felt…something.

Under any other circumstances, she'd have rushed to Dr. Sterling's office weeks ago, and her doctor would have insisted on a diagnostic mammogram, rather than a simple screening.

But much as she'd like to create an alternative reality, one in which she could afford unlimited doctor's visits even without insurance, she couldn't. "No. I haven't seen her."

Since Elizabeth was taking advantage of a program offering free mammograms to uninsured Marysburg residents, Cailyn likely understood the situation without further explanation. At the very least, she didn't ask any more questions.

"All right." Brown eyes kind, Cailyn gave her a reassuring pat on the shoulder. "I'll do my best to get crystal-clear images."

And then the normal routine began. How many times had she had this procedure? Seven? Ten? Definitely every year since she'd turned forty, and Dr. Sterling had ordered at least one baseline mammogram before then. By this point, Elizabeth knew the basics of how to angle her body and her arm, how to lean into the machine when necessary and hold still.

Her left breast compressed between the glass plates, and as always, she noted its resemblance to an unbaked loaf of ciabatta. Dimpled, off-white, and vaguely rectangular.

Two images, like normal. Then the tech helped her switch sides, and her right breast went between the plates. More pressure as they squeezed together once more, spreading her into an even layer as effectively as her favorite rolling pin did pie dough.

Elizabeth tried to concentrate on that vision, letting its familiar sweetness distract her. Rolling out a disc of dough and transferring it into a pie plate. Cutting off the overhang and crimping the edges. Inspecting the little bits of butter within the dough, which would provide flakiness as they melted and steamed in the heat of the oven. Filling the shell with thin-cut apples, tossed with cinnamon-sugar, lemon juice, a few more pats of butter, and a pinch of salt. Weaving a lattice of dough strips for the top and brushing them with cream for extra browning.

From the humid warmth of her mental bakery, she heard

and obeyed Cailyn's gentle directives. Position. Freeze. Reposition. Freeze.

Then Cailyn told her to breathe again, and Elizabeth inhaled deeply, her chest loosening for the first time in weeks. The two standard images of her right breast had been taken. Any moment now, the tech would tell her to put the gown back on and return to the dressing room. She'd don her bra and sweater and find out in a few days that the stupid lump was meaningless, nothing of concern.

This horrible month would have a happy ending, and she could go back to worrying about normal things, like that rattle in her car or whether she had enough extra money to maintain her small monthly donation to Planned Parenthood.

All stressful considerations, of course, but not nightmarish. Not anything that would keep her sleepless for weeks on end, waiting for the next free mammogram event nearby.

But Cailyn didn't smile and say they were done. Instead, she bit her lip. Fiddled with the machine, looking at God knew what on the screen.

Another repositioning, and then the tech took one more image. Two more.

Elizabeth coughed as the pressure in her chest returned and ratcheted tighter.

"Are you okay?" The smile crinkling the corners of Cailyn's eyes had disappeared. "Do you need a minute?"

She didn't need a minute. She needed insurance. She needed her mom. She needed a stalwart barrier between her and a world abruptly turned frigid and terrifying.

"I'm fine." Another approximation of a smile, and then she couldn't help but say it. "Does everything look okay?"

Every year, she asked the same question, and she always got the same answer. The tech couldn't make that determination, and the radiologist reading the images would send a report to Dr. Sterling within five business days.

Usually, though, the tech would seem relaxed and smile in a way that told Elizabeth what she needed to know. The images were fine. She was fine.

This time, however, Cailyn remained silent for several heartbeats before speaking, her lips pressed into a tight line. "Your doctor should hear from the radiologist within three to five business days." Another pause. "Or sooner. The radiologist might have time to look at this today. I'll check with her."

The kindness, the probable reason for it, paralyzed Elizabeth in a way a brusque dismissal wouldn't have.

"Even when she sees abnormalities, most of the time it's nothing. Calcifications or a cyst or something harmless. A simple biopsy can tell you one way or another."

Cailyn's voice had become a little higher, the pace of her words a little more rapid, probably because she wasn't supposed to say any of these things to a patient. But she was young and concerned and not experienced enough to disguise either.

"So don't wor—" The other woman cut herself off. "Anyway, you should hear soon. Let's take one more image, and then get you back into your nice, warm sweater."

Elizabeth was pretty sure she'd never be warm again.

Another slight repositioning, another held breath, and it was done. She walked to the dressing area, her sweater held in front of her exposed flesh like a shield. Behind the cloth curtain, she peeled off the too-tight gown, hooked her bra, slicked on the deodorant stashed in her purse, and pulled the sweater over her head, tugging it past her hips.

Then she braced her hands against the wall and dropped her head to her chest.

After a few minutes, Cailyn spoke on the other side of the curtain, her tone gentle. "Are you okay, Ms. Stone?"

The poor kid had asked that question before, and the answer would be the same. The answers, really.

Not at all. Not for months, and definitely not now.

"I'm fine," Elizabeth said.

LATER THAT AFTERNOON, AS CAILYN HAD promised, the call came.

CHAPTER 2

James glanced at the dashboard clock, the numbers bright green and accusatory in the twilit gloom. Ten minutes to six. Dammit, he was going to be late, and he didn't have time to pull over and call Elizabeth.

That last job at the Keplinger house had taken way more time than he'd anticipated, largely because the new kid on his crew had ordered the wrong damn paint for the living room, a semi-gloss blue instead of a matte yellow. An extra early-morning trip to get the right color and finish had set James behind all day.

He'd intended to shower and change before the town hall. Elizabeth wouldn't protest, of course. She'd never been overly concerned with appearances. And Lord knew he didn't give a fuck what some jackass congressman or his supporters thought about him. But meeting his old friend in a paint-splattered sweatshirt and jeans, his hair plastered to his skull by the wool cap he'd worn during trips outside, pained him anyway.

In their better years, his ex had teased him about it sometimes, how meticulously he tried to straighten himself before they gave final instructions to the babysitter and met Elizabeth—with or without one of her boyfriends—for dinner.

"We lived with her in a tiny apartment for two years," Mel would say, rolling her eyes as he ran a comb through his hair and ironed his shirt. "She's seen you passed out on a stained sofa with dicks Sharpied on your face. I think she can handle uncombed hair."

"That was in our university days," he'd tell her. "Over a decade ago."

What he carefully neglected to add: *Back when I was drinking too.*

Then, behind the closed door of their bedroom, he'd catch Mel by the waist, press her against the wall, and remind her that the only woman he cared to impress was her. All while hoping he wouldn't taste tequila on her tongue.

In their worse years, when they'd moved cross-country and her drinking had become a constant in their lives, their visits home to Marysburg and occasional dinners with Elizabeth had turned fraught.

"You don't prep like this for our other friends." Mel would watch him in the hotel mirror, her mouth a hyphen.

He'd inhale through his nose, struggling for patience. "There was never anything between Elizabeth and me. You know that. You and I were already together when we lived with her."

Mel would nod, but she wouldn't look convinced. At dinner, she'd go through an entire bottle of wine or half a dozen margaritas and try to drum up arguments with either him or an ever-calm Elizabeth. And once they got out to the car, the slurred accusations and screamed invectives would begin.

Finally, he'd stopped suggesting dinner with their old friend and former roommate during visits to Marysburg. Just another way he'd contorted his life, his relationships, everything he did and was, around his ex-wife's alcoholism. But after the divorce, once he'd returned to his hometown for good, he'd called Elizabeth and apologized. Asked for forgiveness and company at their favorite diner that night.

She'd accepted him back into her life without questions or recriminations. She provided pleasant, undemanding companionship when they both had time. She baked him cookies for every conceivable holiday. She was the antithesis of drama, and around her, he could just *be*.

His history, his choices, his regrets: She knew them all in a way no one else did, not even his parents or his sons. Over the years, he'd hidden so much from his family. From everyone.

He'd wanted to shield his kids from pain. Wanted to protect the privacy and sanctity of his marriage. But because of Elizabeth's unique position in his life, she'd witnessed some of the hardest, most horrible moments of that life.

She hadn't flinched. Hadn't done anything but offer understanding and warmth.

So she deserved him clean and kempt, and she deserved him prompt.

Especially since he'd never, not once in almost thirty years of friendship, heard her make such an impassioned plea for company. For support. As soon as he'd read the Facebook DM, he'd told her she could count on him. He'd be happy to attend a damn town hall or a wake or a wedding or whatever. Anything for her. And it wasn't as if he'd miss another long, solitary evening spent reading or watching HATV before trudging upstairs and tumbling into a big, chilly bed.

There. There was the road leading to the high school.

James arrived in the parking lot two minutes before Congressman Herb Brindle's town hall was due to start, wedged his truck into the first available space, and sprinted for the entrance closest to the auditorium. His back ached with each jarring step, just as it did when he made his sad attempts at jogging four times a week, but he gritted his teeth and kept moving.

The foyer contained two or three clusters of people still chatting and four SWAT officers in polo shirts. They eyed him carefully, but he turned away, still looking for Elizabeth's trademark pale blond hair and solid frame.

She was nowhere to be found, probably because the event was due to start any moment and she'd already taken a seat. Hopefully she'd saved him one too.

To his vague surprise, there was no security check at the door to the auditorium, just a taped-up paper that read "NO POSTERS OR SIGNS." Ironic, that. And as soon as he poked his head inside, he saw that glorious hair, glowing beneath the overhead lights like a beacon.

He hustled down the aisle, his boots landing in noisy thuds on the floor. But other than a few more security people around the margins, no one paid him any attention. They were still chatting as they waited for the congressman, who appeared to be filming an interview with a local news reporter at the side of the auditorium.

Elizabeth wasn't chatting with anyone, though. She wasn't even watching the congressman. She was staring at the empty stage, at a spot containing nothing of real interest.

Even when he lowered himself into the seat beside her, she didn't move. Didn't acknowledge him. Was she angry he'd cut the timing so close?

"I'm sorry, Eliz—" he started to say, but then she jerked at the sound of his voice and turned her head in his direction.

Her deep-set blue eyes, usually so clear, were bloodshot, the lids swollen. Her skin had transformed from rosy to blotchy, its paleness mottled by angry patches of pink. Her strong features appeared to have sunken in on themselves somehow, turned creased and saggy when he'd always considered her an ageless wonder.

Only that trademark low blond ponytail was normal, its brightness incongruous. Almost obscene, given the fear and worry etched across her face.

She'd never looked like this. Ever. Not even at her mother's funeral a couple months ago. Jesus fucking Christ, what was going on?

He wrapped a hand around her upper arm, and the chill of her flesh seeped through her sweater. "Are you okay? What happened?"

Out of the corner of his eye, he could see Brindle moving toward the stage. They only had a minute to talk. Maybe seconds.

Her throat shifted as she swallowed. "I'm fine."

A lie refuted by its telling. He could barely hear her, even though the audience had quieted in anticipation of the congressman's words, and her voice was rough in a way he didn't recognize.

Enough. She didn't belong in a damn high school auditorium, not in her condition.

"Let's go somewhere we can talk. Somewhere warm." He got to his feet and held out his hand to her. "My house is closest."

He'd turn on the gas fireplace and crank up the heat until those tiny shivers wracking her frame stopped. He'd swaddle her in a blanket, get her some of that fancy hot chocolate she liked, and make her tell him everything. Then he'd figure out how to fix it, whatever it was.

She took his hand, but only to tug him back down to his seat. "No."

"But you're—"

Her mouth set, she shook her head. "I need to do this."

"You need to do what?"

But it was too late. A woman in a navy dress had stepped up to the mic stand and started yammering about Brindle's accomplishments, his love for his constituents, and a bunch of other shit James neither believed nor cared about.

He leaned over to whisper in Elizabeth's ear. "Are you sure you want to stay?"

Her soft hair caught on his beard, several strands pulling loose from her ponytail. The scent of baking surrounded her in a nimbus, imbued in that hair and the fabric of her clothing. Vanilla and almond and fresh bread. Sweetness and comfort.

She smelled edible. Always had.

At his words, she shivered again, harder. Then she nodded.

After a round of halfhearted applause from the audience, the woman retreated from the stage, replaced by the suit-clad congressman.

Brindle cleared his throat and gazed out over the auditorium. "It's my honor to speak to you tonight at Marysburg High. As you know, my constituents are the reason I'm here, in every possible sense. And tonight, I'd like to share with you some crucial information about our national debt and the dangers of our ballooning deficit before I open the floor to questions."

Beside James, Elizabeth took a shaky breath, her long, blunt fingers curling into fists on the armrests. Without thinking much about it, he covered the hand closest to him.

Her fingers were stiff under his. Cold. But as Brindle ran through his PowerPoint presentation, complete with endless bar graphs and alarming spikes in various charts, they gradually loosened and warmed, flattening against the plastic armrest.

Abruptly, as the congressman seemed to be reaching the

end of his speech, she turned her palm upward, and their fingers intertwined.

Holding hands. They were holding hands for the first time in almost thirty years.

The fit felt natural. Easy, in a way he hadn't anticipated. And her shivers had waned at some point over the last several minutes, which allowed him to take his first full breath in half an hour.

Her distress disturbed him. Immensely. He'd had no clue. Not given her usual self-possession, her seeming imperviousness to damage, the way she'd remained stalwart and cheerful even during the sale of her bakery and her mother's slow, painful decline and death.

Had she been stalwart and cheerful? Or had that been a performance enacted for the comfort of her oblivious audience?

Earlier, she'd told him she was fine when she clearly wasn't. He didn't like to think of her lying to him, and he didn't like to think of how many times she might have done so in the past without him noticing.

Brindle finished discussing his last slide and clicked off the projector. A few audience members, quiet to that point, gave another perfunctory round of applause.

One of the few remaining so-called moderate Republicans, Brindle didn't tend toward fiery speeches or prophecies of doom. His soundbites were reasonable, conciliatory. But he voted with his uber-conservative colleagues every time, no matter how egregious their positions became or how many people—especially women, people of color, and members of the LGBTQ community—their policies hurt.

As far as James was concerned, the man was a fucking coward. Maybe he talked a good game about welcoming immigrants, but he didn't denounce their harassment by ICE or the splitting of families by deportation. Maybe he acknowledged the importance of affordable healthcare for all, but he stood by while the Republicans drafted bill after failed bill that would strip that healthcare from millions.

Brindle was either devoid of principles or lacked the courage to fight for them. Either way: The man was a blight on Virginia and their nation. He needed to be voted out, and soon.

James sincerely hoped someone in the auditorium would ask the congressman where he'd stored his spine, and whether a good ass-kicking would help him find the key.

When Brindle opened the floor to questions, a few audience members raised their hands. Including, to his shock, Elizabeth, the woman who'd bemoaned and feared every oral presentation she'd been assigned in college and never raised her hand in their shared American lit seminars.

This. This was why she'd come, fear of public speaking be damned.

She was shaking again, her fingers squeezing so tight he heard one of his knuckles crack. But she kept her other trembling hand high in the air, gaze pinned to Brindle's nearest roaming flunky with a microphone.

The tie-clad young man—a Young Republican from Marysburg University?—caught her eye, gave a little nod, and headed their way.

Her breath hitched, and her fingers spasmed around his.

When the kid leaned over, his outstretched hand holding the microphone, Elizabeth slowly, clumsily rose to her feet. James expected her to disentangle their hands at that point, but she didn't. And he wasn't letting go until he knew she was okay, whether that happened in a minute or an hour.

So he scooted forward in his chair so she didn't have to lean to the side and held her hand as she spoke into the microphone, her voice quavering.

"My name is Elizabeth Stone, and I'm a lifelong resident

of Marysburg. My question concerns your stance on healthcare." She licked her chapped lips. "I'm very concerned about—"

"Let me stop you for a moment, Ms. Stone." The congressman held up a hand. "I want to be clear that I understand the importance of healthcare to Virginians and all Americans. Every time I hear the story of an innocent child's illness driving a family into bankruptcy, I grieve more than I can say." Lips pursed, he shook his head. "Health insurance needs to be affordable and readily available. But as my presentation just demonstrated, we also have to find a solution that won't bankrupt our government in the long term. That's a tough challenge, but it's one my Republican colleagues and I are more than willing to take on. We'll keep working on it until we find the right answer. For you, and for everyone."

He paused, clearly waiting for applause. When it didn't come, he turned back to Elizabeth. "What's your question, ma'am?"

She was breathing fast, but she didn't avert her gaze from the congressman. After one more squeeze of James's hand, she began talking again.

"Let me tell you a little about my family medical history, Congressman. My Grandma Stone died of breast cancer before I was even born. My father didn't talk about it much, but from what I hear, she had a lump under her arm the size of a grapefruit before she went to a doctor, and by then it was too late. She was dead before my dad even graduated from college." Her fingers had turned cold against his once more. He covered them with his free hand, surrounding her as best he could as she spoke. "Grandma Barker had a mastectomy in her late forties. She survived for a couple more decades before she got lung cancer."

Elizabeth cleared her throat. "Both of them were smokers,

unlike my mom. And my mother never got breast cancer, although she had a few questionable mammograms over the years. My sisters haven't had any issues either. But you can understand why I've always been concerned about breast cancer. Terrified of it, actually."

He'd had no idea. None.

"Last month, I—" She paused. "I found a lump in my right breast while I was showering. But I don't have health insurance, and I wasn't comfortable going into debt to pay for a mammogram."

James must have made some sort of sound, because she stopped speaking for a moment and glanced down at him. With a nod, he encouraged her to keep going, but he barely heard her next few words.

When the fuck had Elizabeth lost her insurance? And why hadn't she said something to him? He could have paid her premium. He could have paid for a fucking mammogram. Shit, he'd have *begged* her to take his money and go to the damn doctor.

They'd been friends for decades. Unlike most of their circle, she hadn't blinked when he'd decided to shift from teaching English to painting houses. She'd tolerated Mel's abuse and tried to stay close to them both, even in the midst of all the alcohol-soaked drama. She brought him homemade soup when he came down with a cold or fever. She baked him cookies for every conceivable holiday—including Arbor Day, for Christ's sake—and fed him basically every time she saw him. He figured he could blame ninety percent of his belly on her, and the other ten percent on the Rita's frozen custard place near his house.

She'd been a steady, supportive, undemanding presence in his life almost as long as he could remember.

And she'd been without insurance and terrified, and she hadn't fucking told him?

No. This was unacceptable. And as soon as this damn town hall ended, he was going to tell her so. Right after he held her until she stopped shaking.

"—and the radiologist said I needed a biopsy as soon as possible, but if I couldn't afford a mammogram, how can I afford a biopsy?" Elizabeth's voice was so shredded now, he could barely make out her words. "And if it's cancer, how can I afford treatment without spending the rest of my life in debt? What if my lack of coverage means I don't get the care I need?"

Even as her tears spilled over, she jabbed a finger in the congressman's direction. "But let's say the lump is nothing, I survive this year, and I try to get coverage next year. If the latest Republican healthcare bill passes, I won't be able to pay for health insurance anyway, because of all my preexisting conditions." She jerked the hand twined with James's against the softness of her stomach. "I'm fat. I smoked for a while in my twenties and have occasional asthma. And since the abnormal mammogram is in my records now, that'll probably disqualify me for an affordable plan too."

For the first time since James had known her, she'd raised her voice. She was yelling now, those blotches on her face standing out in relief against the bone-white paleness of her skin.

"So, yes, I hear you saying that innocent babies born with health conditions shouldn't die, and their families shouldn't go bankrupt. How generous of you." Her trembling lip curled. "But what about people like me? I'm not innocent. I'm a flawed human being, and I've made some bad decisions. Does that mean I no longer have value to you or to our society? Does being fat and a former smoker mean I deserve to d—"

Her chest hitched, and he brought their twined hands to his cheek, desperate to provide some sort of silent comfort.

After a moment, she continued. "Does that mean I deserve to die? Does that mean I deserve to spend weeks or months awake in bed, wondering whether I have a tumor growing from something treatable to something that will cause me a slow, agonizing d-death?" She was sobbing between every word now. "You need to think hard, Congressman Brindle. About people like me. About what you believe. About whether your conscience will allow you to bankrupt and kill an untold number of Americans in the name of the free market and deficit reduction, even as you increase military spending and cut taxes for the wealthy."

The congressman, his brow furrowed, had extended a hand to her. "Ms. Stone, I'm so sorry that your—"

"No." She cut him off without hesitation. "You've gone on record as supporting every one of your party's failed healthcare bills. So I don't want your sympathy. I want your vote. A no on every cruel healthcare plan your Republican colleagues propose. A yes on universal healthcare. If you can't give me both, save your prayers and platitudes for someone who can afford them. And that's all I have to say."

The crowd erupted into whistles and applause, drowning out Brindle's attempted reply.

Elizabeth wasn't even paying attention to the congressman anymore. Instead, she lowered her chin to look at James. "Can we go now?"

Her nose was red and running, her eyes swollen. But her shoulders were straight, no hint of apology evident on her face. The local news stations' cameras were trained on her, but she wasn't flinching away from them or hiding herself.

She wasn't just kind and pleasant and smart. She was fucking phenomenal. A powerhouse of a woman, even in the midst of such pain and fear.

Why hadn't he seen it before?

He stood. "I'll drive us home. We can get your car later."

Without another word, she slung her purse over her shoulder and headed for the exit, James in tow. At her sudden movement, the SWAT guys headed in her direction, but they stood down when they saw she was leaving.

And as James and Elizabeth walked hand-in-hand to his truck, he started formulating a plan.

ABOUT OLIVIA

While I was growing up, my mother kept a stack of books hidden in her closet. She told me I couldn't read them. So, naturally, whenever she left me alone for any length of time, I took them out and flipped through them. Those books raised quite a few questions in my prepubescent brain. Namely: 1) Why were there so many pirates? 2) Where did all the throbbing come from? 3) What was a "manhood"? 4) And why did the hero and heroine seem overcome by images of waves and fireworks every few pages, especially after an episode of mysterious throbbing in the hero's manhood?

Thirty or so years later, I have a few answers. 1) Because my mom apparently fancied pirates at that time. Now she hoards romances involving cowboys and babies. If a book cover features a shirtless man in a Stetson cradling an infant, her ovaries basically explode and her credit card emerges. 2) His manhood. Also, her womanhood. 3) It's his "hard length," sometimes compared in terms of rigidity to iron. 4) Because explaining how an orgasm feels can prove difficult. Or maybe the couples all had sex on New Year's Eve at Cancun.

During those thirty years, I accomplished a few things. I graduated from Wake Forest University and earned my M.A. in American History from the University of Wisconsin-Madison. I worked at a variety of jobs that required me to bury my bawdiness and potty mouth under a demure exterior:

costumed interpreter at Colonial Williamsburg, high school teacher, and librarian. But I always, always read romances. Funny, filthy, sweet—it didn't matter. I loved them all.

Now I'm writing my own romances with the encouragement of my husband and daughter. I have my own stack of books in my closet that I'd rather my daughter not read, at least not for a few years. I can swear whenever I want, except around said daughter. And I get to spend all day writing about love and iron-hard lengths.

So thank you, Mom, for perving so hard on pirates during my childhood. I owe you.

If you want to find me online, here's where to go!

Website: https://oliviadade.com
Newsletter: https://go.oliviadade.com/Newsletter

facebook.com/OliviaDade
twitter.com/OliviaWrites
goodreads.com/OliviaDade

ACKNOWLEDGMENTS

As always, the feedback from my critique partners and friends helped me smooth the rough edges of this story and polish it until it shone. All my thanks and love to Mia Sosa, Emma Barry, and Melanie Ting. And a special thank-you to Erin, who pushed me—multiple times, because I'm lazy and wanted to be done with the freakin' revisions already—to make a crucial scene sharper and more emotionally incisive. You're amazing, lady.

I relied heavily on the help of Cecilia Grant, Sionna Fox, Zoe York, and Lori Carter as I readied this story for publication. I appreciate all the ways you made a process that causes me major anxiety doable, and sometimes even joyful.

My family is awesome, and I love them more than I can readily express. To Mr. D, Little D, and Mom: Thank you for supporting me and believing in me and my stories.

Made in the USA
Middletown, DE
22 August 2019